A QUESTION OF DUTY

JAYNE DAVIS

Manuscript development: Elizabeth Bailey

Copyediting & proofreading: Sue Davison

Cover Design: P Johnson

ACKNOWLEDGEMENTS

Thanks to my critique partners on Scribophile for comments and suggestions, particularly Kim and Jim.

Thanks also to Alpha reader Tina, and Beta readers Cilla, Dawn, Doris, Helen, Leigh, Mary G, Mary R, Melissa, Patricia, Safina, Sarah, and Sue.

CHAPTER 1

ort Frederick, Albany, August 1760
   "Captain Stanlake to see Colonel Harper."

The clerk in Harper's outer office looked up as Jack spoke, and laid a ruler across the ledger he was examining before getting to his feet.

"I think the colonel is available, sir. I will go and check."

Jack dropped his saddlebags over a chair as the clerk left through a door at the back of the office. He'd sent Booth ahead with his trunks to find rooms in the town and get settled in, and he was looking forward to a bath after days in the saddle.

Rather than take one of the seats against the wall, he paced the room, impatient to know why he'd been ordered here while his battalion was still stationed in Fort Niagara. He'd only had time to take in some framed prints of what appeared to be a mansion in England before the clerk returned to show him through to the inner office.

Colonel Harper was somewhere in his mid-forties,

running a little to fat—unsurprising for someone who spent most of his days behind a desk. He stood as Jack entered, holding out a hand in greeting.

"Pleased to see you here, Captain," he said, shaking hands then indicating a chair beside the desk.

"I was ordered to report to you, sir," Jack said, dispensing with the formalities. He'd never met Harper and had heard of him only as a man who knew a great deal about their native allies.

"Indeed." Appearing unoffended, Harper resumed his seat and took a sealed letter from a drawer. "This was forwarded to me from the Secretary at War's office, with instructions to hand it to you in person. You are to return to England with all despatch—I understand that this letter will explain why."

Jack maintained a neutral expression during this explanation, as was usually wise when listening to unknown superior officers.

"Perhaps you should read it before I explain the travel arrangements I have taken the liberty of making for you," Harper went on.

Jack frowned—the direction was in his brother's hand. Breaking the seal, he scanned the contents—Father was ill, and wished him to return before he died.

"Bad news?" Harper's expression showed sympathy, and Jack wondered how much the man knew.

"On the face of it, yes. My father is unwell."

Harper leaned forward. "Forgive me for prying, Stanlake, but you appear to be annoyed rather than distressed by it."

"I received a letter like this two years ago," Jack

explained. "When I reached home, Father had fully recovered."

"Two years…?"

"At least I missed Abercrombie's fiasco at Carillon." He shouldn't complain too much—the French were just about beaten now, and his regiment was only manning a fort, not taking part in Amherst's attack on Montreal. If this letter had come last year he'd have missed the taking of Quebec. "You said I'd been ordered home?" That wasn't usual—last time he'd had to ask his commanding officer for leave.

"Your father's an earl. Connections in high places, I expect." Harper shrugged.

That was the way the world worked—it was a pity, though, that Father had never used his influence, or his money, to get Jack promoted further than captain. Particularly in view of the incompetence of some of his senior colleagues.

"I've arranged a berth on the *Pegasus*, a packet ship sailing from Boston in a week. Lucky, really—I'd arranged for Lieutenant Ffynes to escort my family on the voyage, but he's—"

Family? Escort?

"—been taken ill and won't get there before the *Pegasus* is due to sail. You've got his cabin, and you will make an excellent replacement for him."

"Family, sir?"

Harper nodded with a fond smile. "Yes. My wife and daughters are returning to London, to stay with my wife's brother. Time for the two girls to find husbands; more choice there. They're all eagerly anticipating access to

3

better mantua-makers and so on. Women's things." He waved a dismissive hand.

Good grief—it was bad enough being dragged away from his duty on what would probably be another false alarm. But accompanying three women...?

Harper pushed a packet of papers towards Jack. "Here are the details. I've recompensed Ffynes for the ticket."

Damn—he hadn't enough cash to pay his way across the Atlantic.

"I'm afraid—"

"No, no," Harper interrupted. "Pay my bankers in London, Captain. All the details are there."

Well, Father would have to give him the money first. Most of his meagre allowance for this quarter was already spent, and he needed to keep something back to pay for the rest of his journey.

"If that is all, sir...?"

"Yes, Captain. I hope you do not return to bad news. Enjoy your voyage."

"Thank you, sir."

As Jack strode back into town, his feelings veered between worry that his father really was dying this time, and irritation at the escort duty Harper had just foisted upon him. It could have been worse, he supposed there was less chance of foul weather at this time of year, so he might not spend too much of the voyage being sick.

Booth was in the room he'd arranged for Jack, removing clothing from one of his trunks.

"Don't unpack too much, Booth. We're off to Boston tomorrow, taking ship within the week."

"Back to England, sir?" Booth scowled.

"Is there a problem?" Jack was surprised at this reaction from his usually imperturbable batman.

"No, sir." Booth's expression was wooden.

"Out with it, man!" Jack said, then suppressed a smile as he noticed a dull redness creeping up Booth's neck. "A woman?"

Booth cleared his throat. "Yes, sir. Was hoping to get permission to marry, sir."

They'd be away for three months, most likely, even if Jack didn't linger at home. And if there was one thing worse than no servant, it was a servant in the sulks. He wouldn't have much need of Booth on board ship, and leaving him behind would conserve some of his meagre funds.

"Just unpack what I need for tonight," he said. "I'll see what I can do."

A note to Harper might help. If the colonel was going to impose his wife and daughters on Jack, the least he could do would be to put in a word with Jack's commanding officer to give his servant leave to marry.

Jack watched the wharves and warehouses grow smaller as the oarsmen pulled out into the choppy water of Boston harbour, and resentment swelled again at being ordered home in this way. He suppressed the feeling—if his father really was so seriously ill, he hoped he would be home in time to see him once more.

He turned his attention to the *Pegasus*, moored out in the bay, and squinted as the wind blew drops of water from the oars into his face. To his landlubberly eyes, the ship looked more like a wallowing whale than a flying horse. They reached the lee of the ship and the oarsmen grabbed the trailing ropes. Jack stood and accepted a steadying hand from above as he scrambled up the ladder and onto the deck.

"Welcome aboard, sir." The greeting was from a young man with a weather-beaten complexion. "I'm Sessions, the first mate. You must be Captain Stanlake?"

"I am." Jack shook hands and turned to watch his trunks being hauled up.

"Jenkins is the steward; he'll show you to your cabin." Sessions indicated a short, round man waiting several paces behind him. "We do not carry many passengers, but we generally manage to keep you comfortable. The last few passengers haven't arrived yet, I'm afraid. We will be ready to sail within the hour, if they are aboard by then." He cast a glance at the overcast sky. "We've a fair wind; it would be a shame to waste it."

As the mate moved away to speak to the boat's crew, Jenkins stepped forward. "The cabins are not very big, sir. Which of your trunks do you require on the voyage?"

"The small one," Jack said. He'd arrived yesterday in time to buy a few volumes from a bookshop and the latest newspapers from England—nearly a month out of date. He'd packed everything he needed for the next few weeks into the smaller of his two trunks.

"If you will come this way, sir?"

Jenkins led the way below, into a dining saloon with a large central table, lit at present by a large skylight above, and a few comfortable chairs bolted to the floor at one end. The passenger cabins opened off the saloon—the one he'd been allocated was tiny, and there was barely room to stand beside the bunk while the seaman carrying his trunk squeezed in behind him and placed it on the floor, then brought him a lantern. A table at one end of the narrow space held a bowl and ewer—empty—and had a small chair tucked under it. There were hooks on the wall, and a couple of shelves with bars across the fronts.

Jack threw his hat on the blankets and scrubbed a hand through his hair. Unpacking took only a few minutes—his new books on the shelves, together with a pack of cards and his shaving things and comb, his coat and spare jacket on the hooks. The rest would stay in the trunk, which just fitted beneath the bunk.

What to do now? Not wanting to get through his books too quickly, he settled on finding a place on deck to watch the preparations for their departure. He should enjoy a surface that stayed in one place beneath his feet while he could. There was no sign of the women he was supposed to be escorting, but they were probably settling in to their cabins.

He hadn't been above decks long when Sessions approached him. "I'm sorry to bother you, Captain, but I understand from Jenkins that you have the cabin originally allocated to a Lieutenant Ffynes, who was to be travelling with Mrs Harper and her daughters."

"I believe so." Jack suppressed rising irritation—he could guess what was coming. "Colonel Harper asked me to look out for them. I take it they are the missing passengers?"

A look of relief crossed Sessions' face. "Yes. They were to stay at the Royal George."

"They set off from Albany well ahead of me, I think,

and I came across no ladies in distress on the way. Do you wish me to go and enquire?"

"I would be in your debt, sir. The captain… Well, suffice it to say he is irascible enough at the start of a voyage, without, er…"

"I understand perfectly." Even the best of superior officers could be trying at times.

"Mama, we were supposed to board the ship this morning!" Clara tried hard to keep the exasperation from her voice as her mother removed a gown from one of the large trunks yet again.

"I know, dear, but they will not leave without us," Mrs Harper said, her gaze not moving from the garment she was holding. "Kitty, do you think this will become Clara better than her blue—?"

"Mama, it's a packet boat," Clara said. "They have sailing dates to keep to!"

"Yes, dear, but we are not yet late, are we? Kitty, what about this one?"

Clara rolled her eyes, hoping her sister could talk some sense into Mama. She'd packed her own trunks for the voyage this morning. The small one held her lap desk and books, and Papa's manuscript; the larger one contained the few garments she would need at sea. They didn't have time for Mama to repack everything.

"You must both look your best on the ship," Mama said, for what must be the fifth time today. "I trust Kitty to have chosen her best gowns, but you take so little trouble with your appearance—"

"Mama, I helped Clara to choose," Kitty said, her fingers crossed behind her back at the lie. "What she has packed will do perfectly well. And it is only a small vessel —there will not be many people to see what we wear."

"But this is the most becoming one." Mama held up Clara's burgundy silk brocade embroidered with ivory flowers.

"Then it should not be exposed to the damp, and possibly salt spray," Kitty said, taking the garment from their mother's hands and carefully folding it back into one of the trunks that would be stowed in the hold. "Besides, you do not want us to marry sailors, do you?"

"No, of course not dear. But Clara has got out of the habit of associating with young gentlemen, and—"

"Mama," Clara interrupted ruthlessly. "We have not even sent a message to the ship. For all they know, we have been delayed on the journey and may not arrive for days."

"Don't be silly, Clara. Captain Stanlake will not let them go without us. How lucky that Lieutenant Ffynes was ill; a captain is—"

"When we left Albany, Papa had only just sent for the captain. He may not get here in time." Clara wished she felt her mother's confidence that things would turn out for the best. But Mama had always been like that, despite frequent evidence to the contrary.

"I'm nearly ready," Mama protested. "You must tidy your hair, Clara. For heaven's sake, why do you insist on wearing it in such a plain knot? Mary did Kitty's very nicely this morning. Why aren't you more like your sister?"

Clara glanced at Kitty's glossy black curls dressed

around her head, with a few long ringlets draped over one shoulder. Kitty mouthed 'sorry' with a quick grimace.

"Where *is* Mary?"

"You sent her to ask for tea, Mama." Kitty had far more patience with her mother than Clara had at the moment, but then Kitty was happy to be on her way to London.

Clara bit her lips against the temptation to ask why, if her mother was so concerned about the choice of gowns to wear on board, she hadn't decided during the week or more they'd been travelling. She had, of course, but then changed her mind numerous times.

"Well, never mind now. But Clara, this captain is the son of the Earl of Marstone. It would be a good connection for either of you—"

"I thought we were returning to England for us to make titled matches?" Clara said. The captain must be a second or third son, otherwise he'd be Captain Lord something-or-other. She had hoped she'd have the weeks at sea to herself before having to be polite to a succession of undoubtedly tedious and self-important young men. Men, moreover, who would be attracted to her only in the hope of her uncle giving her a large dowry. A little like the young officers in Albany, many of whom seemed to be motivated more by her father's rank than her appearance or personality. Only Ensign Blake had seemed to have a genuine liking for her company, and he had been killed three years ago.

"You can never have too many suitors, Clara." Mrs Harper finally shut the trunk, leaving the straps for their maid to fasten when she returned from ordering tea. "Your father was quite the catch at the time; it's a pity…"

Her voice trailed off, and she shrugged.

A pity that he was a good administrator who the higher command had the sense to keep well away from action, Clara thought. Marriage to the third son of a baron had been a step upwards, socially, for a woman from the merchant classes, but Anne Morton's hope that her future husband would go on to achieve fame and glory, and possibly a title of his own, had come to nothing.

And now she had transferred her ambitions to her daughters.

"Well, we'll see," Mama said. "We'll go to the ship as soon as we've had our tea."

CHAPTER 2

"*A*t last," Clara muttered, as someone knocked at the door and entered. It would be Mary, with the tea.

It was Mary, but she was empty handed, and appeared rather flustered, with one strand of her grey hair coming loose from beneath her cap. "Begging your pardon, mum, but there's a gen'leman come to fetch you to the ship."

"We had better go down, Mama," Kitty said.

"He's in the parlour, mum." Mary started to fasten the straps on the trunks. Clara picked up their coats and followed Kitty and Mama downstairs.

The man awaiting them was tall and lean, with startlingly blue eyes and wide shoulders in his faded red coat. He wore his brown hair unpowdered, tied back with a black ribbon. He could be upwards of thirty, although his weathered complexion and stern expression might give a false impression of his age.

"Captain Stanlake." He bowed briefly in Mama's direction. "You are Mrs Harper?"

"Indeed, sir. May I present my daughters? Clara, my elder, and Catherine. How good of you to escort us home."

Clara, watching the captain rather than her mother, saw his brows crease for a moment. An unwilling escort? Their being late would not have helped matters.

"I trust you are all well?" he said.

"Yes, thank you, Captain." Mama sat at a table. "Will you sit and share a dish of tea with us? I have already ordered refreshments." She looked around. "Mary? Where is that woman?"

"No tea, thank you, ma'am." The captain made no move to sit. "Your maid said you were packed, so I asked her to supervise the removal of your luggage. The first mate informs me that you are the last passengers to board, and the captain wishes to weigh anchor within the hour as the wind is currently set fair."

Even as he spoke, Clara heard the thumps of heavy trunks being manoeuvred down the narrow staircase. He was very sure of himself, ordering their luggage removed on only Mary's say-so. But they *were* late, thanks to Mama's dithering, so she should not really resent it.

"Oh, so soon!" Mama exclaimed. "I must go and check that Mary has packed everything. Come upstairs with me, girls."

That brief frown crossed Captain Stanlake's face again, and Clara took her mother's arm as she moved towards the door. "Mary will have made sure nothing is left behind." They would be in close company with the few passengers on the *Pegasus* for weeks; it would not do to annoy their escort now. Behind her, Kitty was making a pretty apology for the delay as she followed with the captain.

In the hallway, Clara steered her mother towards the outer door, thankful that she had managed to persuade her to settle their bill after breakfast. If there was a further charge for the tea they'd not had time to drink, the inn had Papa's address.

Outside, the trunks were already loaded on a handcart and being taken down the street, Mary following behind.

"The walk will do us good, Mama." There would be fresh air aplenty in the coming weeks, but little chance for exercise. Kitty moved to Mama's other side and started to talk about the voyage, preventing any more dithering. The captain followed, Clara aware of his silent presence behind them.

The sky was a dull grey, with a hint of rain in the air. Clara shivered, glad she had insisted on packing her old winter calico jacket and petticoat—not fashionable, but much warmer than her other clothes, and its dark green more practical for shipboard life. The cries of seagulls and the salt air had been with them since they arrived in Boston two days ago, but as they neared the water, Clara heard the slap of waves against the jetties. A sea voyage was an adventure, but she was not looking forward to Mama attempting to marry her to a title. The relative freedom of her life as an army daughter in the Colonies was about to change.

Snatches of the women's conversation drifted back as Jack followed them down the street. Mrs Harper's exclamations about being rushed away were soon replaced by the younger daughter's quieter chatter. A pretty thing, Miss Catherine, with her black curls and alabaster skin. It would be no hardship to face her across the dinner table. Miss Harper, too, looked well enough, although her scraped-back hair was a nondescript brown above a rounder face, and she appeared to take less effort with her appearance. The same could be said for him, he thought, glancing down at his coat; he was looking distinctly shabby.

Mrs Harper said something about an earl's son, but was quickly hushed by her elder daughter. He scowled, wondering if Miss Harper had interrupted out of embarrassment, or from a desire not to warn their quarry. If they thought he was a fine matrimonial catch, they didn't have their sights set high enough. He barely scraped by on his allowance and army pay as it was, and he had no desire to encumber himself with a wife.

Once on board, Mrs Harper started to discuss which items would be needed on the voyage, so Jack left Jenkins to deal with her. Already men were climbing the rigging and moving out along the yards ready to set the sails. He found an out-of-the-way place from which to observe the final preparations for sea.

At last the anchor was weighed and the shouted orders lessened as the ship gathered way. Jack walked to the rail, gazing back as Boston and its surrounding hills shrank behind them. The Harper daughters came on deck and stood nearby, also watching the land they were leaving. The colours and shapes of the buildings gradually blended until the town could not be made out at all against the land behind.

Miss Catherine glanced at him over her shoulder and

smiled. Jack decided to accept the implied invitation and joined them. "Are you glad to be leaving?"

"In some ways. This place has been our home for five years—I was only twelve when we came. But it's exciting to be going to London; there will be so many more shops, and the theatre, and pleasure gardens. Mama has told us all about it. And it will be good to see Uncle George again."

Jack didn't enquire about Uncle George; one of them was bound to tell him at some point in the coming weeks.

"Clara didn't want to come back," Miss Catherine added.

"Kitty!" Miss Clara protested.

"Well, you didn't, did you?"

Miss Clara sighed and shook her head, casting a rueful smile in Jack's direction. "I've enjoyed my time here," she explained. "The country is so… so big and untamed. I'm sorry I never managed to persuade Papa to take us any further than Albany."

"You are not looking forward to shopping?"

"Bookshops, yes."

Miss Kitty tutted. "You will make Captain Stanlake think you are bookish."

"I am." Miss Clara kept her gaze on the distant land, her tone matter of fact.

Her sister rolled her eyes heavenwards, but with a little curl to her lips that made Jack think this might be a common, affectionate disagreement between them.

The land was now only a dark line on the horizon, and Miss Kitty turned away from the rail. "Come below, Clara, there is nothing more to see."

Miss Clara looked as if she were about to object, but then nodded and took her sister's arm.

"We will see you at dinner, Captain," Miss Kitty said.

Jack said something non-committal and turned his attention back to the rolling waves as the young women left. The gentle pitching of the deck wasn't too disturbing. If his stomach had not protested at the motion by the time dinner was served, he might risk eating with the company.

Mary knocked on their cabin door an hour later, with the news that dinner was ready for them in the saloon.

"Are you eating with us?" Clara asked. Their maid had taken meals with them at the inns where they'd stopped on the journey from Albany, but had clearly been uncomfortable sharing their table.

"No, miss. I'll be eating with Jenkins and the cook separately, and there's a manservant with the other passengers. You two go on, now. I'll brush down your coats while you're at dinner."

In the saloon, Clara took her place with her mother and sister on one side of the long table. Two other passengers, both men, sat opposite—the older one was rotund, his face lined beneath a grey full-bottomed wig, and his clothing well-fitting, with ornate embroidered trim on his coat and waistcoat. His companion was much younger and slimmer; he had regular features and wore a dark coat with much more restrained embellishments. Some similarity in their features suggested that the two men might be related. Captain Stanlake arrived to take the final place opposite Kitty.

This was a much smaller vessel than the one they had sailed on when they came to the Colonies, and with so few other passengers, Clara thought she might have time for reading after all. And for dealing with Papa's notes.

Jenkins carried in a steaming tureen, its savoury smell filling the air and making Clara's stomach rumble. A crewman followed with platters of buttered bread.

"Broth tonight, ladies and gentlemen," the steward said, swaying gently with the motion of the ship. "While the sea is still flat enough to allow us to serve such things."

Clara tried not to laugh, imagining soup sloshing everywhere as the ship rolled. Glancing at Jenkins, she thought she saw a quick wink before the steward started setting out bowls.

"The captain and mate send their apologies," he added. "The mate will normally dine with you, but both are busy with the business of departure."

"Do excuse me for not introducing myself," the younger passenger said, once Jenkins had left. "I am Jonas Nolan, and this is my uncle, Sir Cedric Nolan."

Sir Cedric nodded, but concentrated on his soup.

Mama made the introductions. "I am Mrs Anne Harper, and these are my daughters. We are travelling home so that they may enter society. My husband, Colonel Harper, remains in Albany."

Mr Nolan's gaze passed over Clara and fixed on Kitty, a gleam of appreciation quickly suppressed. "I'm sure they will be ornaments to society. My uncle and I have been in Boston on business, making new trading connections."

Clara wondered how Sir Cedric had come by his title, if he was in trade. A large loan on favourable terms to someone with the King's ear, perhaps?

"And you, sir?" Mr Nolan turned towards Captain Stanlake, who gave his rank and name but said nothing more.

"Eat up, boy," Sir Cedric muttered, reaching for another piece of bread. "Make a good meal while you can —the smooth seas won't last long."

"Oh, dear, yes." Mama glanced at Clara. "If you remember, eating became quite difficult at times on the way over."

The soup tasted as good as it smelled, and was followed by dishes of poached fish, roast turkey, and vegetables, and they all ate in silence for a while.

"Have you been in the Colonies long, Mrs Harper?" Mr Nolan asked.

"Five years," Mama said. "Before then, my husband was posted to Dublin, and we lived with him there."

"And have you enjoyed your time here? In Albany, I mean." Mr Nolan was looking at Kitty as he spoke, and Clara saw a brief crease of his forehead as her mother replied. But his interest in the conversation appeared to quicken when Mama mentioned Uncle George's surname.

"Morton?"

"Do you know my brother?" Mama asked.

Sir Cedric raised his head. "We do a little business with him. Decent chap, good head for investments."

"He will enjoy entertaining the three of you, I'm sure," Mr Nolan said.

"He is a good brother. Tell me, Mr Nolan, where in England do you live?"

Clara couldn't help but be amused at the adroit way Mama kept the following conversation focussed on generalities and away from business. Papa had discouraged such talk—not that he was ashamed of the connection to Uncle George, but he held that business was not a suitable topic for womenfolk. Mr Nolan's apparent interest in Kitty had not escaped Mama's notice, and she had far higher ambitions for her daughters than a mere merchant's nephew.

"Anyone for cards?" Sir Cedric asked, when sweetmeats and pastries had been cleared away, and a bottle of port placed on the table. "Stanlake?"

"Don't mind if I do." The captain had hardly spoken during the meal, and Clara wondered if his aristocratic background made him look down on people in trade, or if he was merely taciturn by nature. He had been friendly enough when they talked on deck, but that was before he knew about their connection to George Morton. He seemed happy to play cards with them, but there was little else to do.

"I'm rather fond of a game of whist," Mama said. "If you three gentlemen don't mind playing for penny points?"

Whether they did or not, they were all too polite to object, and Clara went to fetch a book and Kitty's embroidery from the cabin she shared with her sister. They retired while the whist players were still engrossed, but a knock on the door interrupted them as they were settling into their berths.

"It's only me," their mother called.

Clara pulled the bolt back and Mama came in and sat on the single chair. "Mr Nolan seems a very pleasant young man," she started.

"Do you think he's a fortune hunter, Mama?"

Mama sighed. "He might be—he did show a great

interest once my brother's name was mentioned. Captain Stanlake is far more suitable, but he had very little to say all evening. You should talk to both of them, girls. You have not been in society much."

"I have been, Mama," Kitty said.

"I don't count those young subalterns you had flocking around you, Kitty. Being able to converse easily with people in all walks of life will stand you in good stead once we are in London."

"Yes, Mama." Kitty gave an exaggerated yawn. "Sorry, Mama, but it won't do for us to have dark circles under our eyes from lack of sleep."

"Oh, no, indeed. Good night then, dears."

CHAPTER 3

*J*ack tucked his scarf more tightly into the neck of his greatcoat and breathed deep of the salt air. The wind had strengthened overnight, and he'd woken to find himself being rolled from side to side in his bunk. He'd enjoyed the coffee that Jenkins brought him, but decided to see how his stomach reacted to the new motion before risking putting more into it.

Yesterday's clouds had cleared, and white foam on the waves glittered in the sunshine. Jack sat on a bench on the windward side of the low structure that supported the skylight to the passenger cabin. Tilting his head back, he closed his eyes, enjoying the feel of the sun warming his face.

"Good morning, Captain."

He opened his eyes to see Miss Kitty facing him.

"May I join you?"

"If you wish." He sat up straighter, looking around for her mother.

"It is not improper, I think, for me to sit with you on the open deck with the crew all around."

"No, I imagine not." He moved down the bench, allowing plenty of space for her to sit at the other end.

"It is lovely to have sunshine, is it not?" she said, sitting half-turned towards him. "The waves sparkle so. Such a welcome change from yesterday's grey weather."

"If one must be flung about, it is more pleasant for it to happen in sunshine, certainly."

She gave a pretty pout at his churlish response, then smiled, her eyes twinkling. "Does the motion upset your digestion, sir? I'm sure it will pass. We Harpers seem to be blessed with strong stomachs."

"Thank you for your sympathy, Miss Kitty." He returned his gaze to the horizon—his incipient nausea receded a little when he could see the movement his insides were feeling.

She chuckled. "Did you enjoy cards last evening?"

"I did, although a better partner would have been preferable." He wasn't sorry to have been playing for small stakes, as he had drawn Sir Cedric as a partner, who had a better opinion of his abilities than Jack did, and Mrs Harper had proved to be an unexpectedly astute player.

"I hope you did not lose too much, Captain. Men often assume Mama will dither over her cards as she does with other decisions."

"Not too much," he admitted, with a wry twist of his lips at his own expense; he had thought that himself. But he had enjoyed the game. If his stomach settled enough to allow him to spend the evenings at cards, this voyage might not turn out to be too tedious, after all.

Jonas Nolan crossed his line of vision, coming to a

momentary halt as his gaze flicked from Jack to his companion. His lips compressed as he gave a quick nod and walked on.

"You would be more comfortable out of the wind," Jack said. "There is another bench on the other side—I believe this skylight contraption is just high enough to shelter you from the wind there."

"I'll survive a little breeze, Captain. Besides, we learned a lot about Mr Nolan at dinner yesterday, and very little about you."

Startled at this blatant approach, Jack's eyes turned to her face. She fluttered her eyelashes with an innocent expression, but she had that little curl to her mouth that he'd seen the day before.

"Are you flirting with me, Miss Kitty?"

"I am attempting to, but you are not making it very easy."

"Hmph." He resumed his inspection of the horizon.

"I have only had the chance to practise on some of the younger officers in Albany," she said, with an expression of regret. "They are not the kind of husband I want."

"That is being very direct. Am I to assume that I *am* the kind of husband you require?" If so, she was going about it the wrong way.

"Oh, no. You would not do at all."

Jack was startled into a laugh. "That certainly puts me in my place."

"May I be honest, sir?"

"By all means. Why stop now?"

"Truly, sir, I did not mean to offend you. It's just that Mama…" She looked down at her hands, as if unsure how to go on.

"I did overhear a comment about my being the son of an earl."

"Mama wants us to be happy, but she thinks that means having titled husbands, or someone with such connections."

"And you do not?"

"Not necessarily. I wouldn't turn someone down because of the title if he met my other requirements."

"That is very open-minded of you." Jack couldn't help smiling—he wondered if she had written a list. "What are these requirements, if I may ask?"

"I want a comfortable, *settled* home where I can grow roses, and a husband who holds me in some affection, at least."

"Roses? That seems very… specific." This was the strangest conversation Jack had ever had with a young lady. Although as they tended to be in short supply in remote forts like Niagara, he hadn't conversed with many recently. He generally preferred the company of his fellow officers, or amenable camp followers for more intimate companionship.

"It doesn't have to be roses," she admitted. "But we have never lived in one house for more than a few years together. I want to be able to make a garden that I won't have to leave before it's developed."

"To put down roots." Jack nodded, keeping his expression serious. "Like a tree. Or a rose bush—lovely, but with thorns." He wondered if that last had offended her, but she giggled.

"I suppose I deserved that."

A movement along the deck turned out to be Miss Clara approaching, book in hand.

"Clara, have you come to join us?" Miss Kitty asked. "Captain Stanlake said I am prickly."

Miss Clara raised one brow. "I wonder what you said to him, then. Good day, Captain."

"Miss Clara." She didn't seem to mind that he'd dropped the formality of addressing her by her surname. "Your sister said only that she wishes to become a tree, and that I am not suitable husband material."

Miss Clara shook her head, but her expression was one of resignation, not censure. "One day, Kitty, you must learn to curb your tongue."

"I thought it would be best to clear the air. Captain Stanlake will be in our company for several weeks, and it would not do for the poor man to feel… hunted… all that time." She turned her head to face him. "Clara does not wish to marry at all."

Clara felt her face heat with embarrassment. Could Kitty be any more direct? Luckily the captain appeared to be amused rather than offended, his smile lightening his normally serious expression into something friendly.

"What are you doing here on the windy side of the ship?" she asked her sister. "It will do nothing for your complexion."

"My complexion will recover before we reach England."

Clara regarded the space between Kitty and the captain—the bench was not quite long enough for three people to sit comfortably.

The captain stood. "If you wish to join your sister, Miss Clara, I can find—"

"No, Captain, pray do not disturb yourself. I fear I would become cold too quickly, sitting here."

Kitty stood. "Thank you for your company, Captain. I will leave you in peace. Please, do not get up."

The captain bowed his head as they left.

"I've been following Mama's instructions," Kitty said, when they had settled themselves on a sheltered bench. "You should, too."

"There's plenty of time for that," Clara pointed out. "Although now you've so subtly announced that I don't want to wed, there seems little point."

"Oh, Clara—I suspect the captain wants to get married as little as you do. You cannot spend the whole voyage avoiding him. He is amusing." Her gaze slid sideways. "But here is Mr Nolan."

Clara looked around to see that young man approaching.

"Good day, ladies," Mr Nolan said, coming to a halt in front of them. "May I join you?"

Clara dropped her book in her lap and slid along the bench until her hip met Kitty's. She gestured to the remaining space. Mr Nolan stepped forward, then paused.

"It will be too difficult for you to talk to both of us," Kitty said, from Clara's other side. "I will leave you together."

"You must be anticipating the delights of London," Mr Nolan said, once Kitty had gone and he was settled beside Clara.

"Yes. Mama has told us much about it, although when we last lived there I was too young to be taken to theatres and other entertainments."

"You have not seen Vauxhall Gardens, then, or

Ranelagh. The latter is considered more genteel, I know, as the higher price of admission keeps out many of the lower orders."

"Mama has described them to us, although it is some time since she has been in London." Fifteen years, more or less, when Clara had been but seven years old.

"The Rotunda at Ranelagh is a splendid sight, and means that entertainments need not be limited by the weather…"

Clara supposed he meant well, and she might have been interested had he described anything that she had not already learned from Mama. Out of politeness, she said a few words in the right places, but didn't bother to pay much attention. A theatre was a theatre, after all, even if the London ones were larger than any she'd been to. But when Mr Nolan started to describe the style of houses in London—as if Boston and Dublin were not civilised—she had finally had enough.

"This has been a most interesting conversation, Mr Nolan, but it is rather cold on deck. If you will excuse me, I should go below and check that Mama has all she needs."

Mr Nolan stood. "Enjoyable indeed, Miss Harper. Do let me know if there is anything I can do to make your voyage more comfortable."

Clara inclined her head as she stood, a sudden roll almost making her lose her balance. She ignored the steadying hand Mr Nolan held out as she headed for the companionway leading down to the saloon.

Jack stayed on deck most of the afternoon, reading some of the time, looking up now and then to see streaks of high cloud gathering and then thickening in the western sky. By late afternoon his stomach felt more settled—so much better that he decided to eat dinner with the other passengers.

The first mate joined them at the table, and Miss Clara and Miss Kitty kept him busy answering questions about the ship and the countries he'd visited. Sessions told a story well, and had a fund of amusing incidents to draw upon. Sir Cedric was concentrating on his food, but Mrs Harper and the younger Nolan were also listening with interest.

Whist was once more proposed, but this time Sessions joined Mrs Harper, Miss Kitty and Sir Cedric. Jack, still not entirely sure his dinner would stay where it should, nevertheless accepted a glass of port from the steward and sat back in his chair to watch the game from the other end of the table. Jonas Nolan began a conversation with Miss Clara. He caught snippets of their words, eavesdropping shamelessly while keeping his eyes on the card players.

"…working on this afternoon?" Nolan asked.

"…father's manuscript... fair copy… publishers in London."

Jack shifted in his chair, turning to face them so he could hear better.

"That is a big task for a young lady such as yourself."

"I have plenty of time," Miss Clara replied. "And I find the subject matter fascinating."

When had Colonel Harper found the time to write a book?

"Military tactics, I suppose," Nolan said.

"Oh, no. He's interested in the customs of our native allies."

Nolan's eyebrows rose towards his wig. "Their customs must be very different from our own civilised practices."

Miss Clara's lips curved, although the smile did not reach her eyes. "Indeed they are. My father is naturally most familiar with the Mohawk people, as he has been based in their lands, but the other tribes in the Six Nations have similar customs."

"What do you find most interesting, Miss Harper?"

She gazed at Nolan for a moment, as if considering what to say, then gave a tiny nod before speaking. "Day-to-day duties are divided between men and women, with the men as hunters and the women responsible for—"

"Which is the natural order of things."

"I was going to say that the women are responsible for farming." Miss Clara didn't seem annoyed at Nolan's interjection.

"Oh, well. But women are better suited to more domestic responsibilities, are they not?"

"That is the custom in Britain, to be sure. However, in the tribes my father has studied, the women are stewards of the land. Although only male leaders take part in negotiations between tribes…"

Nolan nodded—in approval, Jack suspected.

"…those leaders are appointed by the Clan Mothers, and can be removed by them."

Nolan's brows drew together. "It is no wonder, Miss Harper, that our civilisation is so much superior. Such duties are clearly best given to those with the aptitude for them."

Miss Clara smiled—a thin smile, the way his schoolmasters had looked when Jack answered a difficult question correctly. Odd. And strange that she did not appear offended by his patronising manner.

"I'm sure you must be correct, sir."

"Men have more logical brains, after all, and a greater understanding of the world."

Miss Clara had a little curl to her lips, just like her sister's, but Jack couldn't work out what she found amusing. Miss Kitty sounded like the kind of woman Nolan had described, happy to confine her responsibilities to the home. He was beginning to suspect that Miss Clara was not.

"I saw Mr Sessions on deck today," she went on. "He had an instrument, and was looking at the sun. Do you know what he was doing?"

"Ah, yes, finding the longitude." Nolan smiled at her. "That's the distance north or south of the equator, you know."

"How does it work, sir? It seemed very complicated."

To Jack, her expression was too innocent—was she teasing Nolan in some way?

"I… er… It is complicated, Miss Harper. It is to do with the angle of the sun above the horizon, but there is a great deal of mathematics involved."

"Oh, my woman's brain would not understand, then. Never mind."

Nolan appeared to be oblivious to the sarcasm. Miss Clara put a hand to her mouth and coughed, then stood up. "Excuse me, Mr Nolan. I'm afraid I need a drink of water."

Not long after Miss Clara left, her sister got up from the card game. "I must see if my sister is well, Mr Nolan. Please, would you take my place?"

31

Jack opened his mouth to volunteer, but Miss Kitty caught his eye and shook her head as she left the saloon. It was such a small movement that he wondered whether he'd imagined it. But when the two sisters returned a few minutes later, armed with a book and an embroidery hoop, he had to suppress a laugh. Nolan was now safely trapped in the card game where neither of them had to talk to him.

He debated joining them, even though Miss Clara appeared intent on reading, but the deck suddenly lurched beneath him. An accompanying protest from his stomach made him think he would be wiser to lie down in his cabin. His seasickness usually wore off after a few days at sea—unless the weather was particularly rough—but it clearly hadn't quite reached that stage yet.

The sisters loosened each other's laces, then Kitty sat out of the way on the end of the bottom bunk to give Clara room to undress. She didn't move when Clara got under the covers.

"So what did Mr Nolan do to make you interrupt my card game? Mama and I were winning."

Clara drew up her knees and wrapped her arms around them. "Women are not capable of making important decisions. And whatever the topic, he's certain he has more knowledge than me because I am a woman."

"He said that?"

"Not in so many words, but his meaning was perfectly clear."

"That's what most men would say."

"I know." Clara sighed. "I think I'd rather spend the voyage in silence than have to listen to him instructing me. The Nolans do not appear to be in need of money—they have fine clothes."

"That may be why he wants to marry money," Kitty suggested.

"It's possible, I suppose. Captain Stanlake appears more in need of funds. That, or he hasn't managed to find a tailor recently." To be fair, it must be difficult to keep a uniform in good condition in the forested wilderness.

"But his father's an earl; he must be rich."

"If he is, why is he still a captain? I'm sure Papa was a colonel by his age."

"Perhaps he's been cast off by his father, left to fend for himself amidst the wild natives and the horrors of war?" Kitty assumed a dramatic pose, tilting her head back and putting one hand to her forehead, wincing as her elbow hit the cabin wall.

"Serves you right," Clara said, as Kitty rubbed her elbow. "It's none of our business, anyway."

"Mama would like it to be."

"Mama would like many things to be. Now get undressed and go to sleep."

Kitty donned her night shift and climbed into the top bunk, dousing the lantern hanging from the ceiling. Clara listened as Kitty's breathing became slow and regular, envying the ready way her sister could fall asleep at any time. Her mind was full of the tales Mr Sessions had told at dinner—stories of foreign lands that she was unlikely to ever see. Women did travel, but generally only those with wealth of their own.

Captain Stanlake probably had many tales, too. Although he had said very little to her so far, he hadn't had much opportunity, and he'd taken Kitty's flirting and frank comments with good humour. She preferred his more rugged features to Mr Nolan's smoother looks—perhaps she would do as Mama wished and spend some time talking to him.

CHAPTER 4

hen Jack emerged from his cabin for breakfast the next morning, only the Nolans were present. He sat beside them and made polite conversation over the bread rolls and cold meats—the usual platitudes about the current weather, and uninformed guesses about their arrival date in Falmouth.

His food eaten, and a fresh cup of coffee before him, he turned to the newspapers he'd bought in Boston. A fire in the Portsmouth dockyard was the most interesting happening; most of the parliamentary reports were about funding for the war with France.

"Take an interest in politics, do you, Captain?" Sir Cedric asked, as the Harper women arrived and Jenkins set them places further down the table.

Jack put the paper down without regret. "I try, but reports such as these…" He flicked the paper with a finger. "They are written assuming the reader knows what has gone before—it is hard to make sense of some of

JAYNE DAVIS

it when the papers only reach Fort Niagara intermittently, and months old."

"Hmm, it must be. It's not so bad in Boston. Need to follow events, you know. So many happenings can affect the price of goods, and the government could always do more to protect trading vessels. However, there are opportunities aplenty, despite these troubled times, for those with an eye for mutual profit."

Jack wondered if Sir Cedric was about to invite him to join in some trade venture. "My family mostly has income from farming," he said. That wasn't a lie, although Father doubtless had investments in addition to revenues from land rents.

Sir Cedric seemed to lose interest, merely giving Jack a nod and resuming his breakfast. Jack picked up his paper again.

"You should get some fresh air, Clara." Mrs Harper's voice interrupted his reading only a few minutes later. "Perhaps Captain Stanlake would be good enough to escort you?"

"Mama!" Miss Clara's protest, although quiet, was clearly audible, her face reddening.

Nolan had heard, too. "I would be happy to escort Miss Harper, if—"

"No need, Nolan," Jack broke in. He was curious about that conversation between Nolan and Miss Clara at dinner last night. "I'd be very happy to take a turn about the deck."

She glanced at him, then got to her feet. "Thank you, sir. I will see you up there shortly."

He fetched his greatcoat and scarf, and awaited her at the entrance to the companionway. Thin clouds covered the sky, turning the sun to a mere bright patch. The wind was stronger than the previous day, blowing from directly aft and filling the sails.

When Miss Clara appeared, he led the way to the sheltered bench. She did not sit, but stood facing him with her hands clasped together.

"I must apologise, Captain. I would not wish to be foisted on you like this." She met his eyes briefly, clearly still embarrassed by her mother's action. He couldn't tell if the rosy blush on her cheeks was due to that or the cold wind; whatever the reason, it gave her face an attractive colour.

"I would enjoy your company, Miss Clara. However, we may just sit here, if you prefer. I can fetch a book from my cabin, and we need not—"

"No, no, Captain. I have no objection to conversing with you, but Mama…" She took a deep breath. "May I be frank, sir?"

"By all means."

"We are returning to England so that I might meet more people—men, to be precise. Mama has decided that it is time I found a husband."

"That is not unusual, Miss Clara. But your sister has already informed me of this, as well as my peripatetic occupation making me unsuitable as a candidate for her." Or for anyone else, really. He could not imagine himself permanently settled—with or without a rose garden—and what woman would be happy to be left at home when he was posted abroad, often for years at a time?

"Unfortunately, Captain, you are still a potential…"

"Target?"

"Indeed. A potential target in Mama's eyes, due to your connections."

"Ah. My father's title."

"That is *her* opinion." Her gaze met his firmly this time. "I try not to judge a man merely by who his parents are, but on what *he* is."

"That will put me on my mettle," Jack said, hoping to put her more at ease.

"I... I did not mean—"

"Miss Clara, I spoke in jest. Please do not be uneasy about this. If you prefer to talk to young Nolan, you have only to say so."

"No."

He couldn't help smiling at the decisiveness of her denial. "You appeared amused by his conversation at dinner last night. I'm afraid I was eavesdropping for some of it, but it did not seem to be a private discussion."

She sat on the bench, half-turned towards him, but did not speak.

"I found his explanation of navigation particularly illuminating," Jack prompted.

Miss Clara gave a wry smile. "Even I, a woman not suited to the comprehension of complex matters, know that longitude is the distance east or west of Greenwich, not a north-south measurement as Mr Nolan said."

"We should be grateful, then, that he is not in charge of the vessel. And that I am not, either. I wouldn't have the first idea about finding our position."

"At least you do not pretend that you do, sir."

"Or *assume* that I know better because I think I'm superior." Like Major De Lacy. "That can be dangerous."

"Is that the voice of experience?"

. . .

Clara wished she hadn't asked as Captain Stanlake frowned. Scowled would be a better word, really. "I apologise if—"

He shook his head, his expression smoothing. "No need. I was remembering an incident when I was a raw lieutenant, fresh from England. Our Indian allies have been fighting in their forests for centuries, and it requires quite different tactics from those suited to the more open terrain the British army is accustomed to."

"Papa says the local militia fight better than the regular battalions sometimes."

"I have found it so, certainly. A lot depends on the attitudes of the officers. When I arrived in the Colonies, I served under a major who thought that no Indian or militiaman could possibly know better than he how to use his men to fight off a greater number of Frenchmen. He didn't live to regret ignoring their advice, but neither did a fair number of the men. The rest of us were lucky to escape." He met her eyes. "It was a salutary lesson not to pass judgement on others' opinions or knowledge without thought."

"As Mr Nolan did to me, although without such dire consequences. His assumption that women are not capable of taking part in the governance of a tribe was both annoying and predictable. Most men—most people, even—think the same." She wondered if he did, and was only being polite.

"About the superiority of our civilisation? Or the superiority of men?"

"Both. Does the fact that the people in another land do things differently mean we are better than they are?"

He appeared to be seriously considering her question. "Not necessarily, no. But their society doesn't have the same material comforts we do."

"Must that make their society worse than ours? That was Mr Nolan's immediate assumption." Clara awaited Captain Stanlake's response with interest—and some trepidation. He had fought alongside the natives, and she would be interested in learning about his experiences, but not if he had the same disdain for the traditions of others as Mr Nolan. Strangely, she felt that it mattered to her that he did not.

"Their society appears to work well enough, by their standards," he said, after giving it some thought. "I don't know a great deal about the way their tribes are organised, but if they are governed by the gentler… what we call the gentler sex, it doesn't appear to make them any less warlike." He regarded her with a slightly wary expression, as if he were afraid of offending her.

"I do not mind being referred to as the gentler sex, Captain. I am not going to bite your head off if I disagree with something."

"Hmm, no." One corner of his mouth curled up in a lopsided smile. A very attractive expression, particularly when combined with the humour in his blue eyes. "You will be quietly amused, and likely go away and abuse me to your sister."

She denied it, although she had done just that after Mr Nolan's conversation.

"I do regard our society as more civilised, in many

ways," he went on. "In our treatment of prisoners, for example."

She had to agree. Papa had told her that prisoners were often put to death in agonising ways, and she'd been grateful to have been spared too many details so far.

"Clara, there you are!"

Clara bit back a word of protest as Kitty approached. She had been enjoying the discussion. It was a novelty to have an attract— to have any man agree with her ideas.

Kitty was well wrapped up in a coat and scarf, and so had not merely come to summon her below decks. Captain Stanlake stood. "I will leave the sheltered seat for you, Miss Kitty. Miss Clara, it was a pleasure talking to you." He bowed and headed towards the stern. Clara couldn't tell from his expression whether he was relieved or disappointed that their discussion had come to an end.

"Your quarry escaped, Kitty."

Kitty shrugged as she sat beside Clara. "Never mind. He's fun to flirt with because he knows I'm not serious."

And enjoyable to talk to because he knew she was, Clara thought.

The wind rose throughout the afternoon and changed direction, blowing from one quarter and tearing foam from the white tops of the waves. The thickening clouds blocked the sun, and the *Pegasus* heeled over, rising and swooping down as the waves passed. Sessions finally called for men to go aloft to reduce sail.

Jack steadied himself with one hand on the rail, watching the activity. He was fascinated, as always, by the dexterity with which the men swarmed out along the yards with only a rope to support their feet, and wrestled the billowing sails into submission.

About to retreat to the saloon, he changed his mind when Miss Clara came to stand beside him. The sisters had not stayed long on deck this morning after he left them, but here she was again, and in worse weather.

"Miss Clara, is something wrong?"

She met his gaze with a grin, the wind whipping tendrils of hair across her face. "I heard orders being shouted, so I came to see what was happening."

Jack tilted his head towards the west, where the dark clouds were lit occasionally with a flicker of lightning. "A storm."

A sudden lurch made her stagger, and he put out a hand to steady her. She nodded thanks, and peered around him towards the stern. "I guessed as much. How exciting!"

Exciting? "Are you not concerned?"

"Should I be? Mr Sessions is still in charge—I assume he'd have called the captain if there was anything to worry about."

She had a point.

"That may change, of course, but for now..." She shrugged, her grin reappearing as she watched the passing waves; it remained undimmed even when a sudden gust threw spray at them. "I enjoy watching the sea, and the way the ship harnesses the power of the wind. Man battling nature and using it for his own ends."

"Nature frequently wins."

"Oh, do not spoil sport, Captain! My cowering below decks will not make the ship any safe—"

She spun around, ducking behind him and hunching her shoulders just as another burst of spray hit them. Jack swore at the shock—it wasn't merely a smattering of water drops, but felt as if someone had thrown a bucketful of icy water at the side of his head. "You might have warned me!"

"I'm sorry—there was no time." But she was laughing, not contrite. She reminded him of his own exhilaration on a fast ride, ignoring rain and flying mud—although that was usually when he had a proper house to return to, with a hot bath and a roaring fire.

Miss Clara was still laughing up at him when he saw the next dousing coming, and he stepped smartly to one side.

"Aah!" She wiped her face with one hand and shivered. "How ungentlemanly of you!"

"Tit for tat, Miss Clara." He waited with interest to see how she would take it. Her brief pout reminded him of Miss Kitty's flirting, then she licked her lips and grinned. She had a very pretty mouth, in a face glowing with fun. Wet strands of hair stuck to her cheeks and neck, and Jack found himself wishing he could lick the salt from her lips for her. Help her mop up the trickles of cold water that must have got inside her coat.

"Captain?" She sounded uncertain, and he wondered if he'd been staring.

Good heavens—what had come over him?

"I'm sorry, Miss Clar— Watch out!" He acted the gentleman this time, managing to turn so his back took the brunt of the spray, and he felt only a small rivulet of cold running down his neck.

Miss Clara was looking behind them, where the

horizon was now obscured by a grey sheet of rain. "Exhilarating as this is, Captain, I fear Kitty will not be pleased at the prospect of having my wet clothes hanging in the cabin." She ran her fingers under the collar of her coat. "I should go and change before too much soaks through."

"Very wise." Jack followed her down the companionway—the prospect of spending the rest of the day sitting around the saloon table was now more enticing than it had been, although he should not spend too much time contemplating Miss Clara's mouth.

Jack was sitting at one end of the table with a cup of coffee when Miss Clara finally reappeared. She spread out a set of papers at the other end, near where her mother and sister were quietly talking. Making the fair copy of her father's manuscript that she had mentioned a couple of days ago, Jack supposed. He had to admire her ability to wield a pen as the ship moved, although ink stains on her fingers and a handkerchief with black blotches suggested she might not have mastered the art completely.

He'd brought a book with him, but found himself watching Miss Clara instead of reading. Why did he feel more attracted to her than her sister? Miss Kitty was prettier, by most objective standards.

It wasn't because Miss Kitty had denied any interest in him as a potential husband. Miss Clara was determined not to marry at all. Or was she? It had been Miss Kitty who had stated that her sister did not wish to marry—although Miss Clara had not denied it. Miss Clara did have interesting depths, beyond her liking for storms, but trying to work out why one woman was more appealing than another was a futile exercise.

Leaning back, watching the tiny crease between her brows as she concentrated on her writing, he wondered what she would look like if she dressed her hair more loosely. As he watched, she marked places on text already written, referring back through the pile now and then and copying sections from different pages. She wasn't merely replicating the manuscript—she was editing. But now was not the time to ask her about it.

He opened his book, but after only a couple of pages he realised that his stomach had not settled as much as he'd hoped. If he could not be on deck, the only thing for it was to lie down with his eyes closed until the motion ceased.

CHAPTER 5

*A*lthough it was still raining the following morning, the *Pegasus* did seem to be moving more smoothly. When the aroma of coffee drifting into his cabin became appealing rather than nauseating, Jack decided to risk breakfast. He'd spent too much of the night remembering Clara licking her lips, and imagining how she might taste, how she might feel in his arms. And when he'd forced his mind away from that, he'd wondered if a woman who enjoyed watching a storm, and had expressed her regrets at not seeing more of the country than Albany, might not mind a life following the drum. Might even relish it...

But such a match was not possible—not without causing a permanent breach with his father. Although Colonel Harper's birth was respectable enough, the earl would not approve of Mrs Harper's connection with trade.

He put that thought from his head as he took an empty seat in the middle of the long table. Jenkins poured a mug of coffee, then brought him ham and eggs. As he ate, the Nolans began to confer over a ledger and, at the far end of the table, Clara was working on her manuscript.

The ship's motion had eased so much that he decided to attempt to read, and managed to concentrate quite well for an hour or so until Jenkins came into the saloon to ask if anyone required refreshments.

As the steward brought in platters with slices of cold meats and pies, and a fresh jug of coffee, Jack saw Nolan eyeing the empty place next to Clara. Jack stood before Nolan could, and moved down the table.

"Do you mind if I join you?"

Clara started as Captain Stanlake spoke—she hadn't noticed him approach. She had done her best this morning to concentrate on Papa's book, but it was difficult with Mama and Kitty sitting close to her, speculating on what would happen when they reached London. And the captain, sitting further down the table, made her feel… Unsettled, that was it. He hadn't been staring at her, but she'd caught his eyes on her once or twice before he started to read his book. Mr Nolan had glanced in her direction a few times as well, but his gaze didn't make her feel the same way.

"Not at all." She gestured to the place beside her and he sat down.

He glanced at Mama and Kitty, still discussing plans, before speaking in a low voice. "I noticed you were editing your father's work, Miss Clara."

"I… er, yes." There was no point in denying it, if he had

been observing her closely enough to notice. And why should she deny it?

"Does your father know?"

She tried to read his expression, wondering if he disapproved—but he appeared amused. "Not exactly. He thinks I am making a neat copy, correcting spellings and so on. He has sent a letter to Uncle George, asking him to find an editor." She had offered to edit the manuscript herself, but Papa had declined with an indulgent smile that made her grit her teeth. He was a good and kind father, but persisted in his opinion that most women were like her mother, interested mainly in domestic matters.

"Will you give your edited version to your uncle?"

She had been wondering that herself, but hadn't made up her mind.

"It would seem a shame to waste your efforts," he added, taking a bite of pie.

Clara shrugged. "It's an interesting challenge, even if I have to pass it on to someone else. I… It depends on what kind of man Uncle George is—I was a child when we last saw him."

"From the few moments' conversation I had with your father, I suspect he doesn't share your opinion of the… capabilities of women."

"No, he doesn't. I am having to moderate my views on that topic while working." Papa would read the finished book, and she didn't want to anger him by inserting opinions that were too far from his own.

"Should I volunteer to read it when you have finished?" he asked, his face now serious once more. "You will need a man's opinion to ensure you haven't gone beyond the line of what is acceptable."

Clara stared at him in surprise, almost choking as the coffee in her mouth went down the wrong way. His words were so different from the impression he'd given the day before. Then one side of his mouth lifted, and she noticed the laughter in his eyes.

"My apologies," he said. "I see my attempt at humour was unsuccessful. It cannot be amusing to have your abilities continually disparaged."

She shook her head, still regaining her breath.

"I must also apologise for allowing you to get wet yesterday," he went on. "As you pointed out, it was ungentlemanly of me."

A laugh bubbled up at the memory. "No, sir, do not apologise for that. I should not hope to be treated as an equal in some things while choosing to be helpless in others." She hesitated, recalling the idea that had come to her when he first mentioned fighting alongside Britain's native allies.

"I wonder…That is, Papa has a section about how the natives of the Six Nations assist the British army, and others do the same for the French. But Papa has always been an administrator, and it seems a shame to have those chapters written only from hearsay. I wondered if you would read through those parts and check that he has not misrepresented the way things are."

His brows drew together.

"Only if you don't mind, of course," she added hastily. It was not wrong to ask him that, was it?

"I was only thinking that some of it is not fit for a lady's ears." Then he gave that charming smile of his. "Although I'm reluctant to say such a thing to you—and I imagine you have already read those parts."

"Many would say that Papa's whole book is not suitable for females, and I doubt many would read it."

"If it will help, I am happy to do so. Will you—?"

He broke off just as Clara became aware of someone standing beside her. Mr Nolan.

"May I speak to you for a moment?" he asked.

Clara suppressed a sigh, merely inclining her head.

"I'll see if it is still raining," Captain Stanlake said, pushing his empty mug and plate away and getting to his feet. He gave Mr Nolan a nod before disappearing up the companionway steps.

Opposite, Kitty and Mama had fallen silent. Mr Nolan looked at them and swallowed visibly.

"Do sit down, Mr Nolan," Clara said. "I will get a stiff neck peering up at you."

"Oh. Yes, of course." He sat. "I… I wish to apologise, Miss Harper. And to you, Miss Catherine. I think that you have been avoiding my company, and fear I may have offended you."

He *had* lost that irritating air of superiority. But an apology didn't make her more inclined to spend time with him—he would doubtless say something further that would exasperate her. Unless she explained why she'd been offended?

"Mr Nolan—do you think you would make a good soldier?"

He regarded her blankly, and Clara made an effort to keep her expression one of polite enquiry.

"I…Well, no. That life has never appealed to me."

"A sea captain, perhaps?"

"No."

"But you enjoy being a… a merchant. A trader."

"Why, yes. It is a challenge to make new contacts, negotiate prices, predict what customers will…" He tilted his head to one side. "Are you *really* interested, Miss Harper?"

Good—he wasn't totally impervious. "I am interested in many things. However, my point is that you are not suited to the army. Captain Stanlake is probably not suited to be a merchant, or a barrister. Men have different talents and tastes, do they not? Not to mention different abilities."

'They do, yes." He still looked rather puzzled.

"Yet all women, it would seem, must be content to lead a domestic life, and are all suited only for that."

"I did not say… That is…" He cleared his throat and tugged at his neckcloth. "I never had cause to think about it, but I take your point."

"To be fair, Mr Nolan," Kitty broke in from across the table. "I *will* be perfectly content with a domestic life." Beside Kitty, Mama was smiling.

"Thank you, Miss Catherine." He still appeared ill at ease. "I… I must admit to having more than one reason for befriend… For attempting to befriend you both, besides passing the time at sea in pleasant company. Very pleasant company." He nodded to himself. "When I heard you were related to George Morton I… Well, more joint ventures would be good for our business. I hoped that if I could make myself useful during the voyage, that might facilitate a personal introduction to Mr Morton. The only contact so far has been with my uncle."

Clara looked away, feeling rather guilty at the assumptions she'd made about him. He did have a mercenary objective but, to her mind, hoping for an introduction was a long way from trying to marry purely for money.

"I… I am to be married soon," he went on, going a little red around the ears. "My uncle does not entirely approve of my choice, so assisting in a beneficial business arrangement might… might reconcile him."

"Was he hoping you would marry someone else?" Mama asked.

"Nothing had been discussed, Mrs Harper, but there was another company he hoped to make links with."

That, as much as his apology, made him rise in Clara's estimation. He wasn't being mercenary in his choice of life partner.

"Tell me about your betrothed," Kitty said, and Mr Nolan turned in his seat to face her properly.

Clara murmured an excuse and gathered her things together. Captain Stanlake hadn't returned, so it must not be wet outside. This might be a good time to take the air.

Once in her cabin, she stowed Papa's papers safely in their small trunk and pushed it back under the bottom bunk. She took her coat from its hook on the back of the door, but didn't don it immediately.

It was well done of Mr Nolan to apologise—it would certainly make the remainder of the voyage more pleasant now she didn't feel… pursued. She didn't think her comments would really change his view of women, but at least he might manage to avoid irritating her.

How unlike Captain Stanlake, who hadn't made derogatory remarks of that nature at all. He might merely be more diplomatic than Mr Nolan, but if he did share Mr Nolan's views, he hid it well.

Captain Stanlake, too, was probably only befriending

her to pass the time—much as Kitty tended to flirt with young men. She felt flattered that his approach was to take her seriously; that was a greater compliment than any remark about her appearance. There had been that odd expression on his face when they'd been out in the storm, but she should not read too much into that—it was likely due only to cold water trickling down his back.

No, their paths were unlikely to cross again when this voyage was over, so she might as well make the most of his company while they were at sea. When they reached England, he would be off to his father's estate, and she... she would forget him soon enough when she had the sights of London to enjoy and new friends to make. Despite Papa's genteel birth, their families were too far apart in society for them to move in the same circles, even if he were not set to return to the Colonies.

Wishing it might be otherwise was futile.

The rain *had* stopped, and Jack leaned against the leeward rail looking out across the waves. The sea was an unappealing mass of heaving grey water and white foam, but he wasn't really seeing it. He was reliving the feeling that Nolan's interruption had caused. Was it jealousy?

Nolan was only talking to Clara, with her mother present. Nor had she seemed to welcome his intrusion. There was no reason to be jealous of Nolan.

No—his feelings were a passing attraction, nothing more, and would wear off when they parted company. His fancies had never lasted more than a few months—which was just as well, given his circumstances. In the meantime, she was a pleasant companion to relieve the tedium of a sea voyage.

The companionway door opened and the subject of his ruminations stepped onto the deck, bundled up warmly in coat and scarf. She turned her head, and the smile that appeared when she saw him made him feel warm inside. Too warm.

"What did Nolan want?" he asked. Not that it was any of his business, but she didn't seem to mind him asking.

"To apologise." As she explained, he tried to be pleased that Nolan was now in her good graces. It would limit the time Jack would be in her company, but that was probably for the best.

There was a long silence after she finished her tale, but a companionable one, as they both gazed out over the waves.

"Did you mean your offer to help me with Papa's manuscript, Captain?" she asked eventually.

"Why should I not?"

"Your… I mean, working below, looking down at words on a page…"

"You are referring to my weak stomach? It is bearing up well at the moment. It should behave itself now, unless we encounter another storm. What aspects of your father's book are you most concerned about?"

She turned her back to the waves, leaning with her elbows on the rail, the wind blowing strands of hair free from its pins. His hand lifted to tuck them behind her ear, then he realised what he was doing and thrust it into a pocket.

"It's not the facts themselves, but the way he has expressed some of his opinions. He talks about the natives tracking people in the forests, as if they have some kind of animal sense."

"As if they are inferior beings?" Jack made himself concentrate on what she was saying, not how she looked with the wind making her face glow and eyes sparkle.

"Yes."

"As young Nolan did before you… informed him of the error of his beliefs?"

She gaped for a moment, her brows drawing together, then nodded. "Indeed, sir. I find it best to let men know what they should think—it saves them the effort of attempting to work it out for themselves." The twinkle in her eyes belied her stern expression.

Jack laughed, and she laughed with him—she seemed to know when he was not being serious, and responded in kind. That was one of the many reasons he liked her.

"Now could be a good time to start, Miss Clara. Unless you wish to remain above decks?"

It seemed the grey scene had as little appeal for her as it did for him, and he followed her back to the saloon.

Clara accepted the pages that Captain Stanlake handed to her the next morning after breakfast. "What did you think of it?"

He sat beside her. "The facts are correct, as far as my knowledge extends, but…"

"Be honest, please, Captain."

"If I were one of our native allies, I would be offended at some of the things said. It is difficult to pin down—a matter of the choice of wording, really."

JAYNE DAVIS

That was a relief—she'd wondered if she had been reading things into Papa's words that were not there. But this *was* Papa's book, not hers. "Papa...?" How to explain her doubts?

"I suspect you could find a more neutral way of expressing things—one that does not denigrate or praise. The latter would be of no use; readers who already consider the natives as lesser beings will continue to do so, no matter what a book such as this might say."

That was true. Most of the young men she'd met readily accepted the natives as fighting allies, or guides through the forests, but otherwise thought very much as Mr Nolan had. Or as Mr Nolan still did—she suspected he would merely moderate the way he talked about the natives if the subject came up again, rather than her words having fundamentally changed his own beliefs. The captain, though, did appear to respect their allies.

"Did you find it interesting to read?" Once more she felt some trepidation while awaiting his answer—she'd given him one of the sections she had already edited.

"It is a little difficult for me to judge, as I already knew most of what was in there."

That sounded like a diplomatic 'no'. She hoped her disappointment did not show on her face.

"I wonder..." He broke off and shook his head.

"Please, Captain, if you have an idea for improving it, do say so."

"It is not the phrasing and so on that makes it rather... dry, but the information conveyed. All fact, and not much of the people themselves. I wondered if a few anecdotes to illustrate some of the points made might help. I could

56

write some down, if you wish, although my writing style lends itself more to lists and reports."

"I'm sure the subject matter will make it interesting." His conversation was not boring—far from it.

"Do you only wish to edit, or to write yourself?"

How could he know she wanted more than just to make Papa's work readable? Did he know her so well already? "I… I would love to, but have nothing worth writing about. Only the knowledge Papa gathered."

"That might change."

That warmth was in his gaze again, and she looked away before the answering heat within her rose to her face. But he was wrong—if Mama had her way, nothing would change apart from the identity of the man in whose household she lived. She pushed that thought away. For now, editing the captain's stories would be an enjoyable way to occupy the remaining weeks at sea— however unwise it might be to spend so much time with him.

"If we are to work together, you must call me Clara."

"And you must call me Jack."

CHAPTER 6

Falmouth, England, September 1760
Despite the strong breeze carrying spits of rain, Clara and Kitty went up on deck to watch as the *Pegasus* approached the shore. Beside them, Jack was a convenient windbreak as well as a guide.

"Pendennis Castle," he said, pointing to a grey stone building on the low headland to their left. "It was built in Henry VIII's time. There's another fort on the opposite shore." As he spoke, Mr Sessions shouted orders and men climbed the masts to take in some of the sails; others hauled the yards around.

"Do you know this place well?" Kitty asked.

"Not really—the last time I left from here we had to wait several days for the wind to change, so I hired a local guide."

As the *Pegasus* rounded the point, the ships moored in Carrick Roads came into view, then the buildings of Falmouth to their left. The wind eased as they sailed into the shelter of the harbour, and boats were being rowed towards them even before the anchor dropped—to collect the mails, Clara supposed. And for the customs men to inspect the ship. Then it would be time to ferry passengers ashore—but they were to wait on board until Jack had confirmed the arrangements Uncle George had made for them.

Footsteps sounded behind her, and she turned to see Jonas Nolan. "We must say farewell, Miss Harper, Miss Kitty. Although I hope it is only temporary."

"As do I, Mr Nolan." Clara thought of him as an acquaintance, rather than a good friend, but once he'd overcome his condescending manner towards her, they had had some interesting conversations. Clara now knew a good deal more about the trade in fabrics, wool, and cotton. Not that she was ever likely to need the information, but learning anything new was interesting, and she could not concentrate on her father's book all the time. Even Kitty and Jack had taken an interest.

"We travel via Bristol, and my uncle is in a hurry," Mr Nolan said. He glanced over his shoulder to a pile of trunks. "We are to leave as soon as possible, and may manage to get as far as Exeter tonight. I think you would not like to travel so fast."

"No, indeed not." She wouldn't mind—she would be glad to be in Uncle George's house, with a proper bedchamber and a desk that did not move—but Mama preferred to take things at a rather slower pace.

"I… That is, if it is acceptable, I will call on Mr Morton in London next week to see if you have arrived safely."

"Please do," Kitty replied.

"Nolan, may I accompany you as far as the town?" Jack said. "Ladies, I will see you later."

Clara turned her gaze to the water as the two men walked away. Jack had offered to escort them to London, without Mama having to even hint at the request—something she would not have expected from his impatient demeanour when they had first met in Boston. She was glad that they would not be parting company with him just yet. The past few weeks had been…

Interesting? Enjoyable? Both of those, but possibly also unwise. She'd found herself too fond of Jack's company as they discussed the notes he'd made on Papa's chapters about fighting alongside the natives, then the rest of the manuscript. At other times their conversations had varied from serious discussions of literature or places the captain had been to the kind of nonsensical banter that she'd heard him exchange with Kitty on that first day. She'd never enjoyed conversations so much before.

But it was the warmth she felt as they worked together that had really drawn her to him, not only the easy sharing of knowledge. A sense that they had some connection that went beyond mere collaboration.

As the boat with Jack and the Nolans pulled away, Jack's red coat was visible even when the oarsmen and the other passengers were indistinguishable. Resolutely, she returned to her cabin. She checked once more that the bottles of ink in her lap desk were tightly stoppered, then put it into the small trunk with the manuscript and fastened the strap. Mary had already packed their other trunks.

It might have been better if the captain had not agreed to escort them. They had to part at some time, and if he made his own way home from Falmouth, she would have the three or four days of the journey to get used to the idea of not seeing him again. She had begun to wonder what it would be like to have his company always, but an earl's son did not marry someone of her class.

～

Jack slowed his hired horse and let the coach pull ahead as they drew closer to the smoke hanging above London. Tempting though it had been to spend these last few days in Clara's company, he'd chosen to ride rather than share the coach. It was much-needed exercise, after weeks at sea.

He was too used to her company, that was the problem. That would have to end now. The letter he'd sent to Marstone Park from Falmouth would reach there today, if it wasn't there already, and he would be expected tomorrow.

The carriage drew to a halt before a tall townhouse in Cavendish Square. Jack's brows rose—if George Morton owned a house here, he must be wealthy indeed.

A footman rushed out of the house and opened the carriage door, helping Mrs Harper out. She turned to Jack as her two daughters descended.

"Thank you for escorting us, Captain. Will you not come in? I'm sure my brother will wish to thank you in person and give you a bed for the night—you are not intending to ride on this evening?"

"No, I am not." There wasn't enough daylight left, and one more night would not matter. "I would be happy to accept Mr Morton's hospitality."

"Have your trunk sent on tonight," Kitty suggested.

"Then you will not be without it tomorrow when you get home. Uncle George's butler can arrange it for you."

Home? Marstone Park hadn't been 'home' for a decade. But Kitty was waiting for an answer. "An excellent idea, thank you." He had a change of clothes in a small bag —that was all he needed to keep.

"Ah, here is my brother now!" Mrs Harper hurried off, Clara and Kitty following her up the steps to the door where they were greeted by a tall, slim man, clad in sober dark blue. His hair was hidden by a short wig, but the lines on his face made Jack think he was some years older than his sister.

He greeted the women, then Mrs Harper made the introductions. As she followed the butler inside, Morton turned to Jack.

"My thanks for accompanying my sister and nieces home, Captain."

"It was my pleasure, sir." And it had been.

"I understand I have invited you to stay the night?" Morton's expression was one of serious enquiry, apart from a crinkling around the eyes.

"You did," Jack couldn't help but smile in reply. "For which, my thanks."

"I will see about the arrangements, Captain, if you wouldn't mind waiting for a few minutes? My footman will show you to the library."

While Morton went to confer with the butler, Jack took in the marble tiles on the floor, the gilded frame of a painting depicting a merchant ship in full sail, and the ornate plasterwork on the ceiling. As the footman led him along the hall, he glimpsed a rich tapestry on a parlour wall, floral carpets, and furniture upholstered in pale silks. Morton, it seemed, was a very successful merchant, and not hesitant in displaying his wealth.

He stopped in surprise as he entered the room the footman ushered him into. It was a library—two walls were lined with bookcases, and a desk stood in one corner. A pair of high-backed chairs flanking the fireplace looked old and worn, but comfortable. A large globe stood on a tiger-skin rug in one corner of the room.

"Mr Morton will join you shortly, sir." The footman bowed and left, and Jack looked at the bookshelves. In addition to bound copies of various journals, there was a wide selection of classical and more recent plays, novels, and poetry. Taking a few down, he saw the pages had been cut—these books were not just for show.

"Do borrow anything that takes your fancy," Morton said as he entered the room and crossed to the tray. "Can I offer you a drink? This brandy is particularly good."

"Thank you, yes."

It was good—far better than that provided on the *Pegasus* or at the inns they'd stayed in on their way to London. Jack glanced around the room again as he sipped it, then turned back to his host.

"Tell me, is this your taste…" He gestured to the worn chairs and the bookshelves. "…or the rooms out there? It is quite a contrast."

Morton sat in one of the chairs by the fire, and Jack took the other. "The tiger is a reminder of my time in India—that hunt confirmed my suspicion that I was not naturally a man of action. I prefer plainer things to the… the *expensive* decor out there. More restful." He regarded Jack with an enquiring lift to one brow.

"A wealthy merchant needs to *show* he's wealthy?" Jack surmised.

"Correct. Your own family do the same, no doubt, but to advertise their status and reinforce their right to rule."

He supposed they did—he'd never really thought about it. Did Morton resent the upper classes? It didn't seem that he was trying to ape them. But how did Morton know of his family?

"My sister wasted no time in informing me of your background, Captain," Morton said, anticipating Jack's question.

"I'm an army officer, nothing more."

Morton sighed. "Anne is still desirous of her daughters marrying up, as she thinks of it. Clara and Kitty have grown into fine young women since I last saw them. I'll have my days full—over-full—once I start accompanying them to dinners and parties. But they deserve a chance to choose husbands for themselves. Within reason, of course. Are you planning on staying in Town long, Captain?"

"No, I must be off to Hertfordshire tomorrow." He explained why he had been summoned back. "I will need to call at Horse Guards when I have been home, to arrange to rejoin my regiment. I hope I may call then, to see how... how Mrs Harper and her daughters are going on."

"Please do. Would you care to join us at the theatre one evening? I have a box at Drury Lane—Garrick is particularly fine in a new comedy."

"I thank you, I would enjoy that." And enjoy discussing it with Clara afterwards, although he knew he shouldn't. But he would have the voyage back to Boston to get over his attraction to her. "The only plays I have seen recently are amateur theatricals—with the youngest ensigns playing the female parts." He took a sip of his brandy. "I'm afraid they turn tragedy into comedy, whether or not that is their intention."

"Ha, I can imagine."

"Oh, this is lovely!" Kitty exclaimed as she followed Clara into the bedchamber they would share. The beds were not grand affairs, but draped in pretty, light fabrics embroidered with swags of flowers and leaves, reflecting the patterns printed on the wallpaper.

Clara should be pleased to be here, with new experiences ahead and new people to meet, but she felt sadly flat.

She was just tired, she told herself. Being jolted in a coach for nearly four days would tire anyone—apart from Kitty, apparently. Her sister bounced on the bed to test it, then opened cupboards and drawers.

Kitty ran her fingers through a bowl of dried flower petals, spreading the scent through the air. "There's a little dressing room here, with…"

Clara got up to answer a knock at the door as Kitty chattered on. A maid stood outside, with an armful of towels, and Clara stood back to let her enter.

"If you please, Miss, there's hot water coming up for a bath, and your maid asked which gowns you want pressing for dinner."

"My yellow robe à l'anglaise," Kitty said, coming back into the room while Clara was still trying to think. "Mary will know which one I mean."

"Where *are* the trunks?" Clara asked. She had only the small bag she'd used on the journey from Falmouth.

"Mama suggested they stay downstairs. She said it will be easier for Mary to press the dresses as she unpacks them, before bringing them back up here."

"Miss, what shall I say about your gown?" The maid had deposited the towels in the dressing room and was waiting for Clara to make up her mind.

"The burgundy one, please." That was her most becoming gown. Kitty was nodding in approval at her choice. It was only polite, after all, to look their best when Uncle George was so kind as to let them live with him. "You have the first bath, Kitty."

"No—you first. Then Mary will have enough time to try a different hairstyle for you—it's time you stopped pulling your hair back like that. I've got some ivory ribbons somewhere that will go well with your gown. I'll go and find them." Kitty followed the maid out without waiting for a reply.

Clara ran her fingers through her hair—it *would* be lovely to soak in a hot bath while she washed it. And Mama would insist that she dress more like Kitty—she might as well start now.

That was the only reason.

Mary had done well, Clara thought as she regarded herself in the mirror. Her hair was dressed a little higher than Kitty's, and the ribbons woven through it made it look a richer brown than usual. The style reduced the roundness of her face, although her skin showed the signs of too many hours spent on the deck of the *Pegasus*.

Kitty, too, was looking lovely, but then it didn't seem to matter what Kitty wore. Even the sun and wind of the last few weeks had only given her face the lightest of tans.

"Come on, Clara, didn't you hear the dinner bell?" Kitty said. "Mary didn't go to all that effort for you to spend the evening admiring your reflection." She grinned. "Come and show off her efforts to the person for whom it's intended."

"Uncle George," Clara muttered as she followed Kitty down the stairs, ignoring her sister's small snort of laughter.

As they entered the parlour, Mama said something about how nice it was to have all their clothing available again, but Clara wasn't listening. Jack had smiled as Kitty appeared, but his expression changed as his gaze shifted to her. It was still a smile, but there was something more in it—it reminded her of the day of the storm, and how his gaze had made her feel.

She took a deep breath and tried to concentrate on what Mama was saying—something about the theatre, and Uncle George's plans for their entertainment.

Uncle George started the conversation at dinner by asking Jack about his experiences in the army, and Jack kept them entertained for some time with amusing anecdotes of people and places, all adapted to delicate female sensibilities by the omission of any details about battles and injuries. That had to be for Mama's benefit, as he had been more forthcoming when they had talked on the *Pegasus*. She suppressed a sigh as she wondered whether the young men she would soon be meeting would... *edit* everything they said to make it suitable for her feeble female brain.

"...heard much of this before." Jack's words were followed by silence. Clara looked up to find all eyes on her—Mama with a frown, Jack with an expression of amused apology. "I *was* boring you, was I not, Miss Harper?"

Why had she suddenly returned to being Miss Harper? But Jack's head inclined slightly to Uncle George, and she guessed it was because they were now in a more formal situation again.

"Not at all, Captain. I was merely wishing once again that I had seen more of the land than the country between Boston and Albany. Uncle George, did you not visit India some years ago? Will you not tell us something of that?"

If she could not travel to these places, at least she might hear of them from someone who had been there. She listened with interest, allowing the others to ask questions; she would have plenty of time to talk to her uncle later, when Jack had gone. But Mama looked weary, and even Kitty was beginning to droop in her chair. Clara wasn't surprised when Mama stood and announced that she would leave the men to their port. "We will see you tomorrow, Captain," she added. "I'm afraid I am too tired to enjoy a longer evening. I think the girls are, too."

"I will say farewell now, Mrs Harper," Jack said, rounding the table to bow over her hand. "I will be setting off early in the morning."

So soon?

"It has been a pleasure escorting you all. Miss Kitty." He bent over Kitty's hand.

"I do hope you find your father improving," Clara said, as Jack turned to her.

"Thank you. And I wish you success with your… enterprises."

She dropped her eyes at his intense look, and felt the pressure of his fingers on hers, then Mama was shepherding them out of the room.

Such a brief farewell—but what more was there to say? The only surprising thing, really, was that Mama had not pressed Jack to visit them when he returned to Town. It seemed that even she realised there was no future in their… friendship.

CHAPTER 7

$\mathcal{T}$he landmarks along the road from London to Marstone Park were familiar, but rather than welcoming each one that showed he was getting closer to the end of his journey, Jack felt as if they were marking a change to his world. Every trip back was like that, to a degree, but this transition felt different.

Life at Marstone Park was ordered and, to his mind, tedious. The army was little different—in peacetime—but there he had a part to play. His role here as second in line to the earldom had vanished eleven years ago, when his first nephew was born. But today he was leaving behind new friends—for he felt that even George Morton had become a friend, despite their short acquaintance. After the ladies had retired they had talked long into the evening, sharing experiences from their travels that were not suitable for feminine ears. Jack had come away with the impression of a man of education and integrity, who dealt honestly with everyone, and Morton had encouraged him to call next time he was in Town.

And Clara… She had been even more beautiful in that gown, with her hair in curls and entwined ribbons—but her appearance had never been the sole reason he found her attractive. She had seemed subdued, rather than happily anticipating her time in Town as she should be. It was selfish, he knew, but part of him hoped she would be missing him as he was already missing her.

As the gates at Marstone Park came into sight, he tried to turn his thoughts to what lay ahead—to seeing his father and brother again, and his brother's family. The day was warm for September, and he welcomed the dim coolness in the belt of woodland surrounding the Park. Riding along the gravelled drive, he enjoyed the last peace he would have for a while, the silence broken only by the sound of his horse's hooves and the creak of leather.

And rustling in the undergrowth…

Instinctively he reached for his pistol, then forced himself to relax. This was England, and footpads wouldn't lurk here, not within the Park. And it certainly wouldn't be the French or their Indian allies.

There was more rustling, the crack of a stick and what sounded like whispers. He smiled and slid off the horse, smacking it on the rump to encourage it to move on a few paces. Then he crept into the trees and pulled his pistol from his pocket, checking carefully that it was not cocked. A glimmer of white showed that his supposition was correct, and he moved closer.

"Hands up! Surrender!" he shouted, pointing his pistol as he strode towards his nephews. Shrieks were followed by giggles as two small figures emerged from the bushes.

"Uncle Jack! You're home!"

"Hello, Will," Jack said, putting his pistol away. "How are you? And you, Alfred?"

"How did you know we were there?" Will asked.

"You sounded like a herd of cows crashing around in there. Did you know I'd arrive today?"

"No," Alfred said. "We were practising being Indians."

"I think you need to practise a bit more." Jack made his way back to the drive, the two boys following. "How is your grandfather?" That was the main reason he was here, after all.

Will's face fell. "He stays in bed all the time now. Mama says he's very ill."

"He was ill two years ago, but he got better," Jack pointed out.

Alfred shook his head. "That's what I said to Mama, but she said he was worse this time."

"What does your father say?" Jack asked.

"Oh, he's not here. We think he's coming back tomorrow."

"He never talks to us, anyway."

"He went away a few days ago, to London. That's why we're out playing now."

What business did Charles have while Father was ill? It was pointless trying to find out anything more from the boys. Alfred was only eleven, if he remembered correctly, and Will nine. "Well, I'd better get up to the house and see for myself. Are you coming?"

They hesitated—torn between wanting to play and being polite, Jack guessed.

"Never mind. I'll come and see you in the nursery later." He laughed as they scuttled off into the trees, whispering—loudly—to each other to move quietly. He mounted and let the horse amble along the drive, further rustling in the bushes giving away the position of his nephews. Wondering if they were planning on ambushing him, he spurred the horse into a canter. He'd love to play with them, but he really ought to present himself at the house first.

Beyond the trees, he turned into the track that would take him directly to the stables, skirting around the extensive parterre that fronted the house.

"Mr Jack!" The old stable master hobbled towards him, a wide grin on his face.

"Good to see you, Gibbs."

Gibbs took the reins as Jack slung his saddlebags over his shoulder and unstrapped the small bag he'd fastened behind the saddle. "This chap needs to be returned to the Eagle in Hertford."

"Very good, sir."

His greeting indoors was rather more formal. The butler, appointed since Jack left to join the army, didn't have the familiar manner of retainers who'd seen him grow up, and politely informed him that his usual room was prepared, the clothes he'd left had been aired for him and Tindale, his father's valet, would attend him shortly and arrange a bath.

"Is Lady Wingrave in residence?" he asked. The boys had said his brother was away, but it might help to ask his sister-in-law about that before seeing his father.

"I believe she is in the gardens, sir. Shall I inform her of your arrival?"

"Yes, please do. Tell her I will come to her as soon as I've made myself presentable." He ran up the stairs.

. . .

Jack found Sarah sitting in a small wooden pavilion in the far corner of the orchard. Her head was bent over a small embroidery frame, her unpowdered hair dressed loosely, and he thought once again what a good wife his father had chosen for Charles. Whether Charles was a good husband for her was a different matter.

The pavilion was new and surrounded by flower beds that resembled a cottage garden crammed with plants in irregular drifts, quite unlike the formal beds in the main gardens. Most of the flowers had gone now, leaving mainly roses and drifts of pink phlox and purple Michaelmas daisies.

"Hiding, my lady?"

She dropped her frame with a gasp, then a smile. "Jack! You're as bad as the boys, creeping up on me like that!"

"Sorry, I didn't mean to startle you." He pulled up another chair and sat beside her as she placed her embroidery and threads on the table.

"Welcome home, although it's a pity it has to be under such circumstances."

"Father really is dying, then?"

"The physicians think so—it's his weak heart, as it was before. Wingrave summoned several men from London to examine him, but he refused to take the potions they prescribed."

"That was probably a good thing." Jack had little faith in men of the medical profession, apart from the army doctors proficient at sewing up wounds or digging out musket balls.

Sarah nodded. "Yes, although I might have tried to encourage him to take his medicine if they'd all suggested the same thing. They did all tell him to rest, though, and he is."

"That's good." He saw a small shake of her head. "Isn't it?"

"I think he rests because he's tired—that's what Tindale says." She leaned forward and patted his arm where it rested on the table. "He will be pleased to see you; I'm glad you came."

"I nearly didn't," Jack admitted. "After last time, when he was fit and well by the time I got back…" He shrugged. "But he—or Charles, I suppose—got someone at Horse Guards to actually order my return."

"Oh? I didn't know that, but then Wingrave doesn't talk to me much. He's been away for a few days, but he's expected back tomorrow." She looked away, seeming to study the flowers surrounding the pavilion, her mouth drooping. Then she turned back to face him. "I know he's your brother, Jack, but you're nothing like him. The less I have to do with him the better. That's part of the reason for this." She waved a hand, taking in the little garden and the pavilion. "It doesn't suit his notion of suitable surroundings for Lord Wingrave, heir to the Earl of Marstone, so he's not likely to come across me here."

"I'm sorry." Although he'd only spent a few months here in total since his brother had married, it hadn't taken him long to realise that Charles wasn't a man who cared about the happiness of his wife.

"Don't be silly, Jack. It's not your fault."

"I met the boys on the way," Jack said, hoping to lighten her mood. "They were playing Indians in the woods. How are they?"

It worked—her face lit up, and Jack listened to

descriptions of their progress in their studies, and the clever things they'd said. If it had been anyone else, Jack would have soon found an excuse to escape, but Sarah's love for her children was so evident that he listened with genuine interest.

Charles was a damned fool.

Would Clara be like Sarah? She clearly had affection for her family. But wondering about that was futile. It might not be his duty to beget an heir, but it was his duty to marry someone within his own class.

Later that afternoon, a footman found Jack in the nursery on the top floor, and requested his presence in Lord Marstone's room. Jack stood, brushed down the knees of his breeches, and carefully stepped over the ranks of toy soldiers arranged beside the line of books that represented the St Lawrence River.

"But you haven't taken Quebec yet," Alfred complained.

"You haven't built Quebec yet," Jack countered. He indicated an area of carpet. "You need to make a flat-topped hill here. We'll attack in the morning—if you're not supposed to be having lessons."

He pulled the nursery door closed behind him, hearing the beginnings of a disagreement about how to build a hill. Had he and Charles bickered like that when children? He didn't remember, but then he didn't recall playing with his brother often, either. He'd spent most of his free time in the stables.

Expecting a sick-room, Jack was surprised to find his father sitting in a chair by the window, a blanket wrapped around his legs and a glass and decanter of water on a small table beside him. The valet bowed and withdrew.

The optimism about his father's health on seeing him out of bed was dispelled as Jack drew close enough to take in the greyish tinge to his skin, the hollow cheeks, and the tremor in the hands resting on the arms of his chair.

"Hello, Father."

"Welcome home, Jack." His voice was reedy, and too quiet. "I'm glad you've come in time."

In time? Jack was about to protest that his father had some years yet, but thought better of it. Father had never been one to dress up the truth in hopeful lies.

"So am I." In spite of the differences they'd had over the years, he meant it.

"How are you?"

"I'm well." Short of money, as usual, but he wasn't going to repeat that complaint.

"That's good." Father turned his head and looked out of the window, towards the parterres lit by the lowering sun, but Jack got the impression he wasn't seeing them. Finally, he took a long, breath.

"I wanted to tell you I'm proud of you, Jack. The career you've made for yourself in the army."

"Thank you." That was all he managed to say, remembering the furious arguments when he had announced his wish to buy a commission.

"I was worried about the succession," his father went on. "Beyond you and Charles, there was only a very distant cousin. That was why I objected twelve years ago. But now Charles has two boys…"

"Fine lads they are, too," Jack said into the silence.

"Yes. Jack, I was wrong to only buy you a commission

in a foot regiment. It was obvious you would join the army, whatever I said. I could have bought you higher than a mere lieutenant, and in a cavalry regiment."

"Oh, it suited me well, Father. There's not much use for cavalry, as much of the country there is wooded, and it's been fascinating working with our Indian allies." He'd earned his promotion to captain. Becoming a major would have been good, but if he'd achieved any rank higher than that he'd have ended up spending too much time on paperwork.

They could have had this discussion any time in the years since Alfred and Will had been born. But Father was a proud man, not liking to admit to mistakes. Jack rubbed his forehead—he really must believe he was near the end, to make an apology like this.

"That's good. You will be staying for a while, won't you?"

"Yes, sir."

"Good. Ride anything in the stables you take a fancy to, Jack." He fell silent then, returning his gaze to the gardens.

"I'm tiring you too much," Jack said, when his father hadn't spoken for several minutes. But Father shook his head and waved a hand towards the decanter. Jack poured a glass of water and put it in his father's hand, helping him to hold it to his mouth, then put the glass back on the table.

"I'd like to see you married and settled," Father said, when he eventually spoke. "I still don't like to think of you facing death in battle. Charles—well, Sarah's a lovely woman, but Charles always had a wandering eye, you know. Still, a good marriage to a suitable woman would set you up. There's Wellford's daughter—a pleasant girl, I'm told, although a bit of a bluestocking. That would be a useful political alliance."

Wellford? The Marquess of Wellford? "Why would she want to marry a second son?"

"Come, Jack, don't be modest—you're a war hero…"

No—one mention in dispatches did not make a man a hero, but Father was still speaking and Jack didn't want to argue with him.

"…your appearance is well enough…"

Jack's lips twitched, in spite of the circumstances.

"…and you're still an earl's son. I'll leave you a couple of my northern estates—they're not part of the entail. You'll have income from those, but Wellford will give her a dowry."

A vision of Clara's laughing smile came into Jack's mind, and a sense of unease began to grow. "You've arranged this, Father? Without asking me?"

"No, no, not at all. I only mentioned the idea to Wellford, months ago. But Wellford wants to see her married —he's not as decrepit as me, but he's no youngster either. You needn't think the daughter's too old for you, Jack. He married late, and she's the youngest. She must be about five years younger than you—old enough to have got over any missishness."

The daughter of a marquess would be an attractive proposition for most men—so why wasn't she already married?

"Wellford has a pocket borough," his father continued. "It'd be good for both our families to have a voice in the Commons. And it's as well to have more than two heirs in the next generation." He rested his head against the back of his chair and closed his eyes. "I would like to know you were happily married, Jack. Consider the idea, won't you?"

When his father hadn't moved for some minutes, apart from the laboured rise and fall of his chest, Jack silently got to his feet and crossed to the door.

"I think he's sleeping," he said to the waiting valet. Tindale nodded and slipped into the room as Jack left.

CHAPTER 8

Rather than returning to the nursery, Jack went out into the western gardens. He needed peace to think. It wasn't so much his father's ill-health— he'd been expecting that, and seventy wasn't a bad age to go. No, it was his talk of marriage.

As he strolled between the low, clipped hedges, he thought back to the last time he'd been summoned home, two years ago. Father had said something then about wanting him settled, but hadn't persisted, and there'd been no suggestion of a possible bride. He hoped Father wasn't going to demand a promise to offer for the woman —he didn't even want to consider her, as Father had requested.

He stopped by a fountain, watching the fish swimming in the greenish water, then turned back to look at the house. The building was huge, with classical columns adorning the front and a wide flight of steps up to the main entrance doors. Jack remembered Morton's remark about advertising wealth and status, and realised that this

81

was what the proposed marriage was about, too. And the one Father had arranged for Charles. Jack had no idea whether Charles was happy, but Sarah certainly wasn't. If he were to marry, he wanted to be on amicable terms, at the very least, with his wife.

He made his way into the orchard. The pavilion was empty now, and he wandered on beneath boughs of ripening apples and pears. One day, he might take pleasure in settling down and owning productive orchards like this, and farms and gardens, and all the other rewards and responsibilities of land and property. But that day was not yet—not for many years. He enjoyed the life of a soldier, his sense of purpose, and the camaraderie of his fellow officers.

Clara *likes* seeing new places, an annoying voice in his head said. But although her father was Colonel Harper, son of a baron, her Uncle George was in trade. His father would not approve of that match.

If he ever suggested it.

Could he? Did his father's approval matter?

Father hadn't approved of him joining the army, but had come around—even if a decade too late to be useful.

This was not the time to consider such things, not with his father so ill, and he tried to turn his mind to other matters. But when he returned to his room, he found that his trunks had arrived and the footman currently acting as his valet had unpacked his clothing for him. There was also a small trunk set on the floor near the window.

"That's not mine," he said.

"Beg pardon, sir, but it's got your name on it."

And it had—on a flimsy label that had almost peeled

off, and written in a strange hand. Curious, he dismissed the footman and investigated.

The trunk wasn't locked, but held closed with a leather strap. Opening the lid, he found bundles of paper tied up with ribbon, several books, and a lap desk containing pens and stoppered bottles of ink. Clara's desk, that he'd seen so often on the *Pegasus*.

He inspected the trunk and teased off the paper with his name on it, managing to leave enough of the label below to make it obvious that this *was* Clara's trunk, to be sent care of Mr George Morton in Cavendish Square.

Had Clara sent it here?

No—Morton's name and the address were in her hand; the label that had been stuck over it was not. Someone had redirected the trunk here on purpose, and the only people who could have done it were Kitty or Mrs Harper.

Kitty had suggested he send his luggage on—but why would she do this? Clara would be upset when she found her work missing.

He took the bundles of papers out of the trunk and examined them more carefully. They were versions of Colonel Harper's book, but none of them appeared to be the final fair copy that Clara had finished only a few days before they reached Falmouth. She would want them back, but perhaps not urgently. He would write to let her know it was not lost, and take it to London himself in a day or two, to ensure it got there safely.

He had said to Morton that he would call on the family —he should not feel so pleased that he had an excuse to do so.

Clara rubbed her temples as the coach pulled up outside Uncle George's house. The footman let down the step before starting to unload the numerous packages and boxes that were the result of the day's shopping expedition.

She was tired. Tired of traipsing around shops and listening to Mama and Kitty debating the merits of this fabric or that for a dinner gown, whether to buy a hat with feathers or ribbons, which shoes to choose for dancing, for walking. She'd been happy to let Mama and Kitty make many of the decisions for her, as they often did. They had better taste in clothing and colour than she did, and more interest in the matter, too. It was just a pity she'd had to be there while they discussed it all.

It wasn't only that, she thought, as the three of them settled in the parlour with tea and a plate of queen cakes. It was the way Jack had said goodbye last evening—with good wishes, but nothing else.

"Clara? Is something wrong?"

She attempted to smooth the frown from her brow, and shook her head. "I'm just tired, Mama. I will go and lie down before dinner."

"Very well, dear. You do look rather wan. Now, Kitty, what do you think to having a new gown made up from…?"

The parlour door closed on more talk of fashions and furbelows, and Clara made her way upstairs.

What had she expected—or wanted—Jack to say? She'd known from the beginning that nothing could come of their collaboration beyond friendship, and how could a friendship prosper when they were unlikely to meet again?

He had wished her success with getting Papa's book published, though. She would have to discuss that with Uncle George, and it would be well to have the final fair copy ready. Checking that might take her mind off the way she was missing Jack's company.

No-one had brought her small trunk up, so she rang the bell. But the maid, when she arrived, didn't know anything about a small trunk, and nor was it anywhere to be seen when Clara went downstairs to the room where their other trunks were still stored.

She sank onto the lid of her main trunk as a sick feeling settled in her stomach. It must not be lost! Not all Papa's work and her own. But how had it gone astray? She'd had it in her room at the inn the night before they arrived here, and she'd seen the coachman load it yesterday morning. It *must* have arrived in Cavendish Square.

Kitty... Kitty had said something to Jack about his luggage.

She jumped to her feet and hurried to the parlour. Kitty and Mama were still gloating over their day's purchases, and drinking tea.

"Kitty, what did you do with my little trunk?"

Too late, she saw that Uncle George was sitting with them—and was the only one looking surprised. She ploughed on regardless. "Where is it?" She'd thought it odd last night that the trunks had not been brought to their rooms; this must be why. And it meant that Mama was part of the plot. "Kitty, it has Papa's book in it!"

"Don't worry, Clara—I kept back the fair copy. And the captain will return the other papers, I'm sure."

"I need *all* of it, Kitty. Captain Stanlake's things went by carrier—what if it becomes lost?"

"Please do not panic, Clara," Uncle George said, setting his cup down. "It would have been sent with the firm I normally use, and they are very reliable. And I'm sure the captain will ensure it is safely returned." He turned to Kitty and Mama. "Why did you do it?"

"It will give Captain Stanlake an excuse to call," Mama said, with no sign of guilt.

"I asked him to call when he returns to Town, Anne. There was no need for subterfuge."

Mama lifted a shoulder. "We didn't know that when Kitty changed the label. And he would be a good match for Clara."

Uncle George sighed. "A suitor who has to be enticed back isn't worth having."

"He can send the trunk back with a carrier," Clara pointed out, at the same time hoping he would not.

"If he does, you'll know he's not interested and you can stop pining over him," Kitty said.

"I'm not…" She caught Kitty's eye and stopped. That was exactly what she had been doing all day. "Kitty, he's an *earl's* son!"

"Yes, that is Mama's point. But *my* reason for doing it is that you like him, and he likes you."

"The aristocracy don't marry into trade." If only they would… this member of it, at least.

"So that's the only reason you think he won't come back? Not because he doesn't—"

"*Kitty!*"

86

"This is not the time, or audience, for this, Kitty," Uncle George said firmly. "Clara, if the captain is going to send your trunk back, it should arrive tomorrow or the next day. If it does not, I will send a man to enquire. Will that do? Things are rarely lost in transit, you know—you only hear about the few items that do not arrive, not the hundreds that do."

Clara nodded, her mind in too much turmoil to think.

"Come and talk to me tomorrow about your father's book. Kitty, you will go and get the fair copy you referred to and give it to your sister. I will see both of you at dinner."

Glad to be dismissed, Clara returned to her room. For the first time in her life, she wished she did not have to share a room with Kitty. Having her feelings for Jack discussed in public had forced her to face the fact that she liked him too much for her peace of mind.

The next morning—once Quebec had been taken and the boys persuaded to pay attention to their lessons for a few hours—Jack had little to do, so he wandered down to the stables. The sun was shining, and a ride would help to pass the time very nicely.

Gibbs quizzed him about his time in the Colonies, then showed him around the horseflesh currently in residence. Jack duly admired Lady Wingrave's pretty little mare, and the ponies used by the boys. Charles had a fine pair of matched black geldings to pull a phaeton, and several hunters.

"Who is this magnificent beast?" Jack asked, coming to

the final stall. The chestnut stallion was well-muscled and large; bigger than any of the hunters. He looked restless, shifting about in his stall.

"Atlas," Gibbs said. "Lord Wingrave bought him for hunting, but he usually uses the others." He jerked a thumb to indicate the animals they'd just inspected. "Poor chap doesn't get taken out often enough. I ride him for exercise more than his lordship does."

Jack reached out and stroked the animal's nose. Atlas snorted and shuffled sideways.

"D'you want to take him out, sir?"

"Why not?" This was a better mount than he'd ever been able to afford.

Gibbs called, and a groom brought a bridle and saddle. When Atlas was ready, Jack led him out into the yard, allowing him to toss his head against the restraint of the reins before gradually bringing him under control. Atlas skittered sideways when Jack mounted, but although strong, he was far from the worst-tempered horse Jack had ridden.

"I may be a few hours," Jack said. "Does the inn at Over Minster still sell a good ale?"

"Aye, that it does. Give him a good run, sir."

Jack nodded, and kept Atlas to a sedate walk until they were beyond the paddocks and out into the parkland. Then he gave the stallion his head for a while, before trying him over some low hedges and then some more challenging obstacles. Atlas tried to go his own way a few times, but soon worked out that Jack was in charge.

An hour later, and after a circuitous route that wound through fields and woods, he dismounted outside the Royal Oak. The ale *was* still as good as he remembered, and three pints later he set off back again, content with life for the present. Good ale, a splendid mount, a sunny afternoon... what more could a man ask?

A woman to warm your bed, that voice said as he rode through the final belt of woodland. One particular woman. An evening of banter with the Harper sisters before taking Clara to...

"Haaah!"

Atlas lurched sideways at the sudden screech, and Jack came abruptly out of his reverie. A small figure danced in front of him, waving a long stick.

"Surrender!" Will shouted, brandishing his spear.

Jack put his hands in the air; Atlas was tired enough to be controlled for a short time with only his legs. "I have no weapons, oh brave and noble warrior." He took hold of the reins and patted his mount. "Well done, Will. You surprised me that time."

Will threw the spear aside with a grin. "I expect you weren't paying attention, sir."

"Possibly," he admitted. "Would the mighty warrior like a ride to the stables?"

"On Atlas?" Will's eyes went round. "Yes, please."

Jack pulled the lad up to sit before him. "Where's Alfred?" he asked, urging his mount into a walk.

"He's doing some extra lessons. Papa says he has to know more because he'll be the earl one day."

"Poor lad."

Will shrugged. "He doesn't think so. He says he's better than me because I'm not going to be Lord anything."

"Hmm. Like me, eh?" He remembered Charles saying something very similar twenty years ago.

Will turned his head. "I'd rather be like you, Uncle Jack."

"Very polite, Will," Jack said with a chuckle, although the lad's smile showed he meant it.

"Do you like Papa's horse?" Will asked, patting the animal's neck. "Papa doesn't take him out very often."

"He's a good ride," Jack said. And wasted on his brother, from what Gibbs had said.

"Papa says he wasn't trained properly."

"He told you that?"

"No. He was angry with Gibbs. I was hiding in the stables and heard him shouting." Will sniggered. "I think Papa had nearly fallen off."

That sounded like Charles. A failure must be the animal's fault, or the servant's—anyone's but his own. He hoped the boys weren't going to take after their father.

"Oh, Mama's there." Will waved happily, and slid off Atlas' back as Jack drew rein in the stable yard.

"Your father's back," Sarah said, ruffling Will's hair. "Go and get cleaned up."

CHAPTER 9

*J*ack handed the reins to Gibbs and offered Sarah his arm to walk to the house as Will dashed off. She no longer had the carefree air of yesterday, and she set a slow pace as if reluctant to return.

"Wingrave should sell that horse," she said. "But he won't admit that he can't handle it. I hope he didn't see Will up in front of you."

"Why?"

"He told Will the animal was dangerous, so…" She shrugged.

"So he won't be pleased that Will has ridden on him without incident," Jack finished for her.

"He's jealous of you, you know."

"Me? Why? I'm merely a captain in a regiment of foot. He'll have the title and the wealth, and he values those things."

"And you don't?"

"Oh, more money would undoubtedly be useful, but

not the responsibility that goes with it. My duty to the regiment and my men is sufficient."

"That's partly it, you know. Your father was so proud when you were mentioned in dispatches, and scours the *Gazette* for news of any actions you might have been involved in."

"He'd do the same if Charles was away for long periods," Jack pointed out.

"Not all feelings are rational."

That was true. "You are very wise."

"It helps to understand what other people are thinking or feeling," she said. "Particularly when their behaviour can have a great effect on me and my sons." She patted his arm with her free hand. "It's a pity he's not more like you."

Startled, Jack stopped and looked into her face, but the droop to her mouth made clear she was not attempting to flirt with him.

There was affection between them, he thought, but that of a brother and sister—not the meeting of minds and friendly teasing in Clara's company that he was already missing. "You're a good mother," he said, at a loss for how to comfort her.

"It's not so bad," she added, releasing his arm as they entered the house. "I do have the boys. He seems happy enough with two sons, and doesn't bother me often now. He finds his own... entertainment... in the village, and his mistress in Town is only half a day's ride away."

Watching her walk away, Jack vowed that he would not marry where there was not mutual liking and esteem, at the very least. And the idea that intimate relations with Cla— with a future wife would be 'bothering' her was anathema to him.

. . .

That afternoon, Jack paused outside the door of his father's bedchamber. If Father was asleep, he didn't want to wake him by knocking. He couldn't hear anything when he put his ear to the door, so he lifted the latch quietly and pushed it open a little way. Footsteps sounded, then Tindale appeared and gestured him back out into the hall.

"I'm sorry, sir," the valet said in a low voice, following him out and pulling the door closed behind him. "Your visit yesterday tired him too much, and Lord Wingrave has just been to see him."

"Is he sleeping now?"

"Yes, sir. The physician has been called." Tindale's grave expression suggested that this was not merely normal tiredness.

"Does he normally get out of bed for visitors?"

"No, sir. But he was determined not to greet you lying down." The valet shuffled his feet. "I wanted to send for the physician yesterday, but he wouldn't allow me to."

"You should have come to me, or to Lady Wingrave."

The valet shook his head. "That might have made him worse, sir."

"Being disobeyed?"

The valet nodded. Jack didn't ask what was different now, but it was not good news. His father was either ill enough to know that he needed a physician, or he was so unwell that Tindale had done it without his consent.

"Does my brother know how bad he is?"

"Yes, sir. I… I had to send him out."

Charles wouldn't have liked that—Jack had to admire the valet's care for his master.

"Keep me informed, Tindale. I will stay in the immediate grounds until he... I mean, I will not be far away. Send someone for me if he is well enough to see me."

"I will, sir. Thank you. Er... Before he left, Lord Wingrave said you were to... I mean, he requested that you see him in the library." The valet bowed, then let himself silently back into the earl's bedchamber.

Jack ran a hand through his hair—he could not leave the Park now, not even for a brief visit to London. If he sent a groom with Clara's trunk, she would have it by this evening. He tried to ignore the disappointment he felt at not being able to deliver it in person.

And Tindale had been very diplomatic—Charles had undoubtedly given a command, not a request.

Charles was seated before the fire in the library when Jack arrived. "You got back in time, then," he said, not getting up.

"It's good to see you, too, Charlie," Jack said. "It was just as well I got a direct order to return."

"You doubted my word?"

"Last time I was summoned back, Father was on the mend by the time I arrived," Jack pointed out.

"It was your duty to return; you shouldn't have needed an order from Horse Guards."

Jack wished he hadn't mentioned it. Trying to make allowances for Charles' natural worry about their father's illness, he said nothing more, but poured himself a glass of brandy and sat down. Charles hadn't been particularly friendly last time he was home, but now he seemed actively hostile.

"And Father didn't even thank me," Charles mumbled into his glass. "After all the effort I went to."

He took a long drink, and Jack wondered how much he'd already had. The decanter was less than half full, and surely the butler would have kept it topped up?

"You tired Father too much yesterday, Jack. He hardly managed to speak to me when I got home, and he didn't even thank…" He broke off and shook his head, as if realising he'd already said that. "You should have waited to see him."

"He sent for me," Jack said. He'd been ordered back to England to see his father, and Charles was expecting him not to do so?

"You made him ill!"

Jack pressed his lips together against a retort. He couldn't argue with the fact, but Charles seemed to be implying that he'd done it deliberately.

"And you can leave my horses alone, too," Charles added.

Startled, Jack paused with his glass halfway to his mouth. "Atlas? Father told me I could ride anything in the stables. The animal was in need of some exercise."

"He's my mount."

"All right, if you say so." Charles was angry enough already, without Jack irritating him further. In any case, he'd promised to stay close to the house, so he wouldn't be riding anywhere for a few days. He left his drink unfinished and walked out of the room—he had Clara's trunk to see to.

. . .

Charles' presence suppressed conversation at dinner. The food was as plentiful as on the previous day, but Sarah hardly spoke a word.

"Were you away on business?" Jack asked eventually, feeling the need to break the uncomfortable silence.

"Of course I was!" Charles scowled. "You don't think I'd be away for anything else when Father is so ill?"

Sarah looked up. "I'm sure Jack didn't mean—"

"Really? You know what he's thinking, do you?" Charles turned on his wife. "I've done my best to do what Father wants, and now he's too ill to even talk to me properly. Thanks to Jack exhausting him yesterday." He jabbed a finger in Jack's direction.

"I was attempting to take a brotherly interest, Charlie, that's all," Jack said, trying to deflect his anger from Sarah.

Charles gestured to a waiting footman to refill his glass. "I saw you two walking together. Keep away from my wife, Jack. Some women are silly enough to be attracted to a man in a red coat, but—"

"Don't be ridiculous, Charles. I was talking to my sister-in-law. It would be rude to ignore my hostess."

Sarah was gazing at her plate, her face red and lips pressed together. Charles' accusation was insulting to both of them. He hadn't finished his meal, but with Charles in this mood it would be better for everyone if he were elsewhere. He folded his napkin and placed it beside his plate. "Excuse me, I have some letters to write." He didn't look at either of them as he left. Sarah would understand his apparent rudeness, and he didn't care what Charles thought.

He was still hungry, so he asked a footman to get a tray sent to his room. After that, he would find something to read, but as he ascended the stairs, he heard footsteps and turned to see Charles stalking across the hall towards the library.

Ah, well. It might be time to brush up his skill at billiards while he had access to a decent table.

The next morning, Clara chose not to go with Mama and Kitty on another shopping expedition. Instead, she asked for a maid to accompany her while she visited several of the booksellers in Paternoster Row and St Paul's Churchyard. As a result, she spent several pleasant hours browsing the various showrooms, and came away with enough books to keep her occupied for a month. And she hadn't yet explored Uncle George's library.

She had her chance not long after she returned, when a footman asked her to go to her uncle as soon as convenient. On entering the room her attention was caught by the floor to ceiling shelving filled with books, and she only turned towards Uncle George when he cleared his throat.

"A woman after my own heart," he said. He was laughing at her, but kindly. "Make free of the place while you are here, Clara. But I summoned you here because this arrived earlier." He held out a letter, the seal already broken.

Jack's hand—she recognised it instantly, suddenly breathless. It was addressed to her uncle, as was proper, and was brief, stating only that he had her trunk safe and would deliver it in the next few days.

'Deliver it', not 'have it delivered'.

"It seems that Kitty's machinations have worked," Uncle George said. "Do you think it wise to see him again?"

"I… I don't know." Her happiness dissipated. "Probably not."

"But you wish to do so, all the same. Do sit down, my dear."

They sat in the chairs by the fire, Clara with her hands in her lap ready for the lecture she knew was coming. But her uncle surprised her.

"Your father wrote to me about finding an editor and a publisher for his book."

"Yes, he told me he had done so."

"Explain, if you please, why the loss of the original materials would be so upsetting. Kitty assured me this morning, when I questioned her, that you had finished the fair copy."

Did he regard women in the same way that Papa did? And Mama, come to that. Uncle George was Mama's brother.

"Is what you have more than a fair copy, perhaps?" He looked amused, rather than censorious.

"I… Yes, I edited it. Papa is rather… long-winded." Her eyes narrowed. "But I do not find that amusing, Uncle."

"I am not laughing at the idea of you improving the work, my dear, merely at the various… deceptions, shall we say? Deceptions carried out by you and Kitty, for differing reasons."

Kitty had meant well, she supposed, and she felt that her own deception was for a good reason. "Yes, I did deceive Papa, but that was merely letting him assume I would only make a fair copy." But Papa was typical of many men. She made an effort to keep her tone reasonable as she continued. "If men would only recognise that women have brains that are capable of thinking of more than fashion and children, I would not have needed to do that."

He shook his head. "Not all men share those views, Clara. I have become as successful as I have partly by using talent where I find it. A lad born in the gutter, but with intelligence and passion, is more useful to me than some scion of the aristocracy reduced to attempting to earn a living—if he even soils his hands by dabbling in trade."

"And a woman? Would you do business with a woman?" She was happy to find that Uncle George had similar views to her own, but how far did he take them?

"Women are hampered by property laws, as well as the attitudes of many men—and women. However, a number of women run successful shops, for example, or inns and schools."

"But not trading ventures or manufactories."

"Some do, but usually by taking over their husband's business when they are widowed. But I see no reason why they should not start businesses of their own, given sufficient training in matters of finance, and so on. Is that what you want?"

"No." She took a breath and looked away. "I mean, I don't know what I want—and that is because I've never really been given the opportunity to consider anything but marriage and having children."

"You don't want to get married?"

Clara could almost hear 'not even to Captain Stanlake?' running through her uncle's mind. "I do want that—

marriage and a family, I mean. If I find the right man." She tried to ignore the thought that she had already done so. "But I enjoyed editing Papa's book, and I was fascinated by what I learned from it, and what Ja— Captain Stanlake told me about his experiences with the natives." She shrugged. "I like learning new things."

"Hmm. I can ask my acquaintance if any of them have a connection to the Blue Stockings Society—although I understand their discussions are limited to literary and artistic matters, rather than other cultures or trading."

Her, a member of the Society? "I'm not sure I have knowledge enough for that." She shouldn't turn down the offer, though, not after the complaints she had just made.

Uncle George waved a hand at the bookshelves. "Work on it, then. I gather that several members publish essays and other works; start by reading those."

"I will, thank you."

"As for your father's book, would you like me to look through his originals and compare it to your edited version? I'm afraid you may need the assistance of a mere male when dealing with publishers, unless your father wishes to pay for copies to be printed." His smile robbed the words of any sting.

"He was hoping to be paid," Clara said. "I... I did have something like that in mind, which was why I was concerned when the original manuscript went astray."

"Very well. We will do that when Captain Stanlake arrives with the trunk." He paused at the sound of voices in the hall. Mama and Kitty had returned, judging by the excited chatter and fragments of instructions about parcels and packages. "I suspect we will be required in the parlour for tea shortly, but do feel free to use this room if you wish to read in peace."

"Thank you, Uncle." But after Jack's note, and Uncle George's understanding, she felt much happier than she had that morning, and was perfectly willing to spend time admiring the latest purchases.

Later in the afternoon, Jonas Nolan paid a call and stayed talking for nearly half an hour. They described their respective journeys from Falmouth, and Kitty and Mama told him of their plans for dinners and visits. He finished by asking if he might introduce his intended to them, and they agreed to meet in the Park the following afternoon for a walk. It wasn't until after dinner that a knock on the front door heralded the arrival of Clara's trunk, accompanied not by Jack but by a groom with a letter.

Clara tried to hide her disappointment, but didn't think she'd succeeded very well.

"He has good reason, I think," Uncle George said, reading the letter and then handing it to her. It said only that his father was very ill, and he could not leave Marstone Park, but he hoped to call when he was able.

"He does," she admitted. The earl must have taken a sudden turn for the worse. Well, Uncle George had suggested several things to do to pass the time, and she had her father's manuscript to check through once more before she took it to a publisher. Those activities might stop her missing Jack's company too much—that was something she should aim for.

CHAPTER 10

*J*ack spent the next few days being where his brother was not. He'd seen his father once in that time—Tindale had come to tell him that Lord Marstone was awake and asking for him. Jack had sat by his bed and talked about his time in the army, not sure whether Father had fallen asleep or was still listening. On his way out, Tindale had whispered that his lordship seemed to be sleeping more easily.

The weather continued fine, the air warm for the time of year, and he'd have liked to take long rides around the countryside. But he'd promised to stay close, so he spent some of his time reading, and the rest with his nephews. When the boys were not doing lessons, they pestered him for more details about battles he'd been in, and eventually he recruited a couple of grooms and the estate carpenter, and they all went off into the woods to build a small fort. The thing was only a few yards across, but they had fun designing it and then working out battle plans for attacking and defending it.

"Captain Stanlake? Sir?" The voice was some way off, but Jack stood up and dusted leaf mould from his breeches. He'd been attempting to creep up on the fort without being spotted.

"Over here," he called.

"Captain, you're wanted back at the house." The footman stopped and gasped for breath. "His lordship…"

"I'm on my way," Jack said. "Alfred, Will, best get yourselves inside and cleaned up. You may be wanted, too."

"Is it Grandpapa?" Alfred asked.

"I expect so." He couldn't think of anything else that would necessitate such an urgent summons. "Quickly, now."

"Tindale says his lordship's taken a turn for the worse, sir," the footman said, as Jack hurried after him. "He's asking for you."

Tindale was waiting by the door to his father's chamber and ushered him straight in. Charles was already there, sitting beside the bed.

"Jack's here now, Father," Charles said, his voice calm but his expression far from welcoming.

Jack sat down at the other side of the bed, in a chair placed ready. "Father," he said, taking the old man's hand.

"I'm glad you came back, Jack," Father said, his voice thin and his words slow. "Promise me you'll marry—I was happy with your mother. I want… I want you to be, too."

"I will, Father." Some day. An image of Clara's face came into his mind. "Soon."

Why did he say that?

"Good, good." Father's voice was weaker still. "Charles?"

"Yes, Father?"

"You're the head of the family, now… We've a proud name. Take care of everyone, my boy."

"I will."

"You'll do well." Father said, after a long silence. He closed his eyes, and his lips curved up slightly. Then his face gradually became slack and his breaths, quiet in the still room, became further and further apart.

"Goodbye, Papa," Jack whispered, using the childhood term. The words almost choked him. He'd seen death aplenty on battlefields, and drowned his sorrow at the loss of good friends with wine and brandy, but this was different. This was the passing of someone who'd always been there, even if half a world away.

Eventually Tindale approached with quiet tread. Jack glanced at him, then placed fingers gently at his father's throat. He could feel no pulse.

"I'll see to him, sir," Tindale said. Charles got to his feet abruptly and went to gaze out of the window. Jack headed for the gardens, in no mood to speak to anyone.

Jack sat up straighter in his chair as the Marstone family solicitor coughed loudly and took a sheaf of papers from his satchel. Everyone in the room stopped talking and an expectant hush descended. It was time for the will to be read.

In the week since his father's death, his two sisters and their husbands had arrived, together with their offspring. The funeral had been held and Father was now entombed with his ancestors in the crypt below the village church.

The week had been tedious, to put it mildly. Charles

had supervised all the arrangements himself, but had made it clear that it was not seemly for Jack to ride around the countryside, nor to distract the boys from their lessons. Jack had spent a little time exchanging news with Honora and Aurelia, but he had little in common with his sisters any more, and their husbands were interested only in hunting or gambling.

"The Last Will and Testament of Richard George Stanlake, 7th Earl of Marstone," the solicitor started.

At least the man didn't drone, Jack thought, as he listened to the obvious passing on of the entailed property to Charles, as the new earl.

"...gifts to family members..."

Jack's interest revived a little as his sisters were left sums of money.

"... and to my son, John, I leave the estates at Kirkthwaite and Nethburn, in Cumberland and Northumberland respectively, to be given into his possession on the occasion of his marriage."

What?

Jack sat up straight, catching a smug glance from Charles. He hadn't expected such a condition, but then he hadn't expected much at all. The requirement would make little difference, other than ensuring he would have enough income to keep a bride when he fulfilled his promise to Father. Luckily, Father had not made him promise *when* he would marry. Or whom.

The solicitor was working his way through a list of servants, each receiving money and a small keepsake as thanks for loyal service. Finally it was over, and the family dispersed to rest or partake of the refreshments laid out in the dining room.

"Come into the library," Charles said, as Jack was about to make his escape. Jack sighed, but did as he was asked. He'd managed to avoid his brother for most of the week, but he ought to let him know that he'd be heading for London the following day. It was time he made arrangements to rejoin his regiment.

"Want one?" Charles asked, pouring himself a brandy and waving the decanter at Jack.

"No, thank you." Jack wondered at his brother's satisfied smile. He seemed remarkably cheerful for a man who'd just buried his father.

"You asked where I'd been on business," Charles started.

"Did I?"

"You did. I'd been to see the Marquess of Wellford, at Father's behest."

Jack didn't like the sound of that.

"I believe Father discussed your marriage?"

"He did, yes." Jack was wary now.

"I've negotiated the contracts with Wellford. They're all ready to sign. It's a pity Father didn't live long enough to see you wed, but he did know at the end that I'd arranged everything the way he wanted it. I've done well for you, Jack."

"Marriage? With Wellford's daughter?"

Charles' smile faded. "Yes, who else would I discuss with Wellford?"

"I'm not marrying a woman I've never seen." Jack tried to push the memory of Clara to one side. The notion of marrying someone he hadn't even met was unthinkable, and he would not have agreed to Charles' proposition even if he hadn't got to know Clara.

"Arranged matches happen all the time."

Yes, and look how yours has turned out.

"You'll have time to get to know her before the wedding." Charles frowned, any hint of satisfaction gone. "And you promised father to wed—I *heard* you. I thought you'd want this."

"I promised to marry. Lord Wellford's daughter wasn't mentioned." Not in that conversation. He knew that was who Father had in mind, but he *had* also said that he wanted Jack to be happy.

"Well, it's all arranged; you can't withdraw now."

"It's not withdrawing if it's something I never agreed to. If you truly thought I wanted the match, then I thank you for your efforts—but you should have consulted me first."

"There wasn't time. Father was dying."

As he'd thought—Charles had arranged it in an attempt to please their father. How strange that both of them had grown up thinking Father favoured the other. "Was that all you wanted to see me about, Charles?"

"Marstone to you, now," Charles spat. "I'm the head of the family, remember? Show some respect."

Jack resisted the impulse to give an exaggerated bow. Coming into the title had really gone to Charles' head.

"It's your duty to marry well, Jack. This will increase our influence, through Wellford's pocket borough. I've done better for you than Father did for me—Sarah's only a viscount's daughter. Besides," he went on, his smug expression returning. "I've just sent a notice of your betrothal to the *Gazette*, and Wellford's expecting you to call to sign the documents."

"You sent—? You did that without even asking me if I

was willing?" A gentleman could not call off a wedding once the announcement was public. Jack took a deep breath; shouting at Charles wouldn't help. "What made you think I'd agree?"

Charles gaped at him. "The prestige—the connection to a marquess. And money. She comes with a hefty dowry, and you'll get two of the northern estates when you marry her. It's a shame to split up the family's holdings in the borders, but we'll be gaining from the connection."

"The estates were left to me when I marry. The will did not specify my bride."

"Can you afford good lawyers?"

Of course he couldn't. "You know the answer to that."

Charles' triumphant sneer made him want to plant a fist in his brother's face. That would be no help—other than a momentary relieving of his feelings—so he took himself out of the way of temptation, merely slamming the library door behind him as he left.

Newspaper—Charles had sent a notice to the *Gazette*. Jack didn't have many options, but if the announcement was printed he would have no choice at all.

Charles said he'd sent the notice this morning. Jack sprinted up to his room; whether it had gone by messenger or in the post, he needed to get it back. It didn't take him long to change into riding clothes. Money—he might have to go as far as London. He cursed when he realised how little coin he had, but it would have to do. Saddle bag, pistols, a change of linen, shaving kit, card case—that would be sufficient if he had to be away overnight. He headed down the servants' stairs so he didn't run into Charles on the way.

"Messenger went off half an hour ago, sir," the stable

master said, when Jack questioned him. "Was told to take it to London."

"Saddle a horse, now."

"Yes, sir."

"No, wait! I'll do it. You didn't see me." Atlas was the fastest horse in the stables, but Charles was vindictive enough to turn the stable master off if Gibbs saddled the animal for him. This way, Gibbs could deny all knowledge.

Some of Jack's energy must have transferred to Atlas, for the stallion was restive, and Jack wasted a few minutes calming him before he managed to get a saddle on and adjusted properly. Then he was off and galloping down the drive.

Sense returned as he passed through the gates, and he slowed the horse to a canter—even Atlas could not keep up that pace long enough to catch the messenger. The roads were busy with carts and carriages, but Jack had little difficulty passing them. That meant the groom would make good speed, too, unfortunately.

He was nearly at Ponders End before he saw a rider ahead that looked like one of his father's—now Charles'— grooms, dressed in the same dark green as the Marstone Park footmen. Jack slowed Atlas to a trot while he debated what to do. Even if Charles wasn't expecting a written acknowledgement that the notice had been received at the *Gazette*'s offices, he would eventually find out that it had not been delivered.

Waiting until a couple of carriages had passed in the opposite direction, he kicked Atlas into a gallop and called on the rider to stop.

"Captain?" The groom's expression was politely enquiring.

"I need the message you're carrying. There's been a mistake. My... That is, Lord Marstone sent me. The new Lord Marstone."

"I'll take it back to Marstone Park, shall I, sir?"

"No. I'll take it."

The groom held it out. Jack broke the seal and found, as he'd hoped, that there was a separate sheet with the wording of the announcement enclosed. He pulled his notebook and pencil from a coat pocket and scribbled on the back of the covering letter. "Here—if Lord Marstone asks you what happened to the message, show him this." His note might prevent the groom being punished for relinquishing it.

The man took the letter, touched his hat, and set off back the way he'd come. Jack watched him go, debating what to do next.

Lord Wellford. He had to see the marquess, and the sooner the better. Father had spoken of his friend several times, and Jack recalled that his principal seat was somewhere in Yorkshire. But one of the boys had mentioned Charles being in London. Lord Wellford would be at his town house, and it shouldn't be too difficult to find out where that was.

He rode on, pondering duty as he went. Duty to his family, his regiment, his country. And his own happiness. They overlapped, but with Charles' idea of what was due to the family, he could not satisfy them all. Not if it meant tying himself to a woman he'd never met.

And when he wanted someone else.

Did he still have a duty to marry within his class?

Charles would have said so. But if he submitted to this demand, his brother would continue to try to order his life. He didn't understand why Charles would want to. He owned the land for tens of miles around Marstone Park, not to mention an estate in Devonshire and several in other parts of the country. And now he had the title, and a voice in the Lords. What more power did a man need?

Jack gave up trying to work it out—he'd never really understood what drove Charles. Was he really jealous, as Sarah had suggested? Of an impecunious captain of foot?

Whatever the reason, he would not live his life at his brother's whim. If he had enough income to support a wife he would ask Clara to marry him—but he didn't.

CHAPTER 11

*I*t was early evening when Jack arrived in Grosvenor Square. Marstone House would be closed up, but Father always kept a skeleton staff, and there might be a butler or footman who knew where Lord Wellford lived when in Town. Failing that, there would be some kind of guidebook in the library.

He didn't bother trying the front door, but rode around to the mews. As expected, the Marstone stables were deserted, but he gave a coin to a groom further down the mews to look after Atlas until the Marstone staff opened the stable, and entered the garden through the back gate.

"Master Jack?" The old footman who answered his knock gaped in surprise, then stood back to allow Jack to enter. "We wasn't expecting anyone, sir; the house is all closed up and Mrs—"

"Don't worry about that… Patterson, isn't it?"

A slow smile spread across the man's face. "Fancy you remembering, sir. Captain, I should say."

"I'm only here for the night. I need to see the Marquess of Wellford, as soon as possible. Do you know where his London house is?"

"It's just across the square, sir. I believe he *is* in residence." Patterson's gaze ran from Jack's head to his boots. "I can open the butler's room for you to use, sir, if you wish to wash before you call. I'll have water put on to heat right away." He eyed the small bag Jack had put on the floor by his feet. "If you let me have your boots, I'll polish them while you change."

"I hope you're good with a clothes brush, too," Jack said. "I've only a clean shirt and neckcloth with me."

Half an hour later, Jack discovered that his efforts to smarten up had been in vain. Lord Wellford's butler was welcoming enough, and appeared to recognise his name, but unfortunately his lordship had gone to his club for the evening and was not expected back until the early hours.

"It is a matter of urgency. What time would be suitable for me to call tomorrow?"

"His lordship should be able to see you at eleven o'clock, sir. I will inform him that you will call then."

Jack lingered in the gardens in the middle of the square rather than returning to Marstone House. It would only take quarter of an hour or so to walk to Cavendish Square, but he should not see Clara until he'd extricated himself from the proposed match with Lord Wellford's daughter. He might find old army comrades in one of the clubs, but he wasn't in the mood to explain why he was here.

He set off eastwards. A meal first, then paying a few shillings for a place in the pit at the Royal Opera House or Drury Lane might help take his mind off things.

~

Clara sat down beside Uncle George as Kitty went to the front of the box with Miss Templeman, both exclaiming at the size of the theatre and the ornate decorations. Mr Nolan's intended was a pleasant, if rather shy, young woman. Her brother had accompanied them, and stood at the back of the box with Mr Nolan, talking quietly together. Then the play started, and they settled down to watch, seemingly oblivious to the noise and chatter still coming from the people in the pit below.

Clara did her best to concentrate on the performance. Theatres and bookshops had been two of the opportunities that had reconciled her to returning to England, but *The Tempest* had never been one of her favourites amongst Shakespeare's plays. She always wished Miranda would show some spirit, and be treated as something other than... well, a possession to be married off to her father's advantage. Fortunately, she was not in that position, but many women were.

She sighed—she couldn't help thinking that her irritation with the plot would not be nearly so marked if Jack were beside her in the box.

"You seem distracted, Clara." Uncle George kept his voice low. "It is only five days since I saw the notice of the Earl of Marstone's death in the *Gazette*. Captain Stanlake will have duties—there is the funeral, the will to be dealt with, and so on."

Clara sighed. Uncle George was too perceptive. But he was also right—she should not expect to see Jack so soon

By the time the fourth act was coming to a close, Clara had resorted to watching the audience in the galleries and the pit. There were as many people carrying on conversations as there were listening to the actors. Not only conversations, but flirtations and arguments. Then her eyes came to rest on a man in the pit—she could not see his face, but something about the way he stood felt familiar. He appeared to be watching the play, but his head didn't turn as the actors moved across the stage.

He looked like Jack.

Then he turned his head as the people beside him started an argument, arms waving, fingers poking chests.

It *was* Jack.

He was in London, and he had not come to see her. Or had he called in Cavendish Square after they left for the theatre? She should not assume the worst—that he was *not* going to call.

"Is that Captain Stanlake?" Uncle George must have noticed her fixed stare.

"I think so." She did her best to keep emotion out of her voice, but Uncle George was a perceptive man. She hoped Kitty and Mama had not noticed—she didn't want to have to listen to their speculation about why he was in the pit instead of a guest in their box.

"I'm sure there will be a good explanation," her uncle said. "He will probably call tomorrow."

Yes—concentrate on that thought. But even as she made that resolution, he looked up, directly towards her, then immediately turned away and started to push his way through the press of people crowding the pit.

The hope that he was making his way to their box faded when no-one knocked on the door, and had vanished entirely by the time they made their way out to the carriage after the play finished.

≈

Jack was not in the best of moods when he was finally shown into the correct office at Horse Guards the next morning. He'd woken hours before his appointment with the Marquess of Wellford, and decided to start the process of returning to his regiment rather than continue to brood on what Clara must think of him.

He was sure she'd seen him in the theatre last night, and he'd promised to call as soon as he could. But not today, not until he'd seen Lord Wellford. He'd started to write a note to say he had business to deal with before he was free, but she deserved more of an explanation than that.

The clerk rose from his desk as Jack entered. "Captain Stanlake, how may I help you? This office normally only deals with serving officers."

"I *am* a serving officer," Jack protested, as he sat down. Muddled orders were nothing new, especially in the heat of a campaign, but there should not be such difficulties here.

"I have your records here, Captain. They show you resigned your commission two months ago." The clerk opened a folder on his desk and leafed through the documents within it.

"I was in Fort Niagara two months ago," Jack explained, attempting to be patient with the man. The misunderstanding was not necessarily his doing. "There must be some mistake."

The clerk shook his head. "No, no mistake." He held out a paper. "It was done by proxy."

Jack took the letter, his hand almost shaking with fury.

Charles—it had to be. The letter told him little more than the clerk had said; it was not in Charles' hand, but it was his signature—as Lord Wingrave, on behalf of the Earl of Marstone, requesting that the matter be expedited. Charles must have done this at the same time as he'd arranged for Jack to be ordered home.

Jack slapped the letter onto the desk. "I knew nothing of this, and I do not wish to sell out. I came here to make arrangements to rejoin my regiment."

"Oh, dear, this is most irregular." The clerk did look regretful, and Jack reminded himself that the situation was not the man's fault. "I'm afraid that will not be possible, even if you purchase another commission. Your position in your regiment has already been filled—orders to that effect have been sent."

Jack clenched his jaw, trying to control his temper. "The money from the sale of my... my *previous* commission can be used to purchase another."

The clerk consulted another paper in the file. "The orders to accept this sale came from the highest levels, Captain. I'm afraid I do not have the authority to deal with this, even if you were to give me an immediate draft on your bank."

That sounded as if Charles had taken the money. He had not mentioned it, but after his machinations around Jack's proposed marriage, it shouldn't have been surprising.

"Who do I need to see about this matter?"

"Mr Porter, I think, but he is currently in Scotland. He is expected back late next week."

Jack stood abruptly—he was accomplishing nothing here, and he needed a brisk walk to cool his anger before meeting Lord Wellford. Losing his commission might turn out to be the least of his worries. "I will write to make an appointment."

The look of relief on the clerk's face as Jack left the room would have been almost comical in other circumstances.

Lord Wellford's butler showed Jack into a parlour overlooking the gardens behind the mansion. The marquess was, as Father had said, of a similar age, but although the joints in his hands were gnarled and his face lined, his eyes shone bright with intelligence, and there was no sign of a tremor in his limbs as he rose and gestured to Jack to sit facing him.

"I'm pleased to meet you at last, Captain," Lord Wellford said. "My condolences on your recent loss."

"Thank you, my lord." Jack took the seat indicated.

"My daughter will be with us shortly—she did request that she meet you before giving her final agreement to the match. After that, I will have my secretary bring the settlements and so on here for you to look through before you sign them. He will explain the details and make any changes you require. Hopefully not too many; your brother negotiated well on your behalf."

"I…" Jack cleared his throat and started again. "I'm sorry, my lord, but matters are not… not as you think. And it would be better if Lady… if your daughter did not join us at this moment."

Poor woman. Not only to be bargained away like this, before even meeting him, but then to have the arrangements cancelled.

Lord Wellford's brows drew together. "Captain, what is my daughter's name?"

"My brother didn't tell me." He could have asked, but it hadn't seemed relevant as he wasn't going to marry her.

"And you didn't bother to enquire?" Icy didn't come close to describing Lord Wellford's tone. It did, however, indicate that the man had some feeling for his daughter.

"The situation is not—"

"Ring the bell, if you would be so good." It was an order, not a request, and Jack rose to pull the cord next to the fireplace. If he was about to be ejected from the house, his problem would be solved, although he'd hoped to be able to explain himself first.

"Ask Lady Elizabeth to wait until I send for her," the marquess said, when the butler appeared.

The butler bowed and withdrew, and Lord Wellford turned his attention back to Jack. "Your brother assured me that this match would be to the benefit of both our families, in addition to suiting you and my daughter."

Damn Charles.

"My lord, I had no knowledge of the existence of your daughter, let alone the proposed match, until a few days ago."

Lord Wellford glared at him, and Jack felt an unaccustomed impulse to wriggle in his chair. Gradually, the glare turned to puzzlement.

"But how is this? Marstone—your late father, that is—spoke to me about the possibility months ago. I understood your brother was making the arrangements on your behalf while you were still abroad, preparatory to you resigning your commission."

"My father did mention it to me a few days before his

death, but only in terms of your... of Lady Elizabeth being someone of whom he would approve. I made no promise about Lady Elizabeth, nor did he ask it of me. I had no idea that Charles was negotiating settlements with you until he informed me of the fact yesterday."

Lord Wellford's gaze pierced him again, then he shook his head. "A bad business, this. It seems that your brother has taken too much upon himself."

That was putting it mildly. "Yes. He also had my commission sold without my knowledge or permission. I have no intention of leaving the army."

"It does seem a trifle... underhand..."

It was downright dishonest, as far as Jack was concerned.

"...but you might still consider the match, Captain. A political alliance between our families would be to the advantage of both."

"I would not do Lady Elizabeth the dishonour of marrying her when I... while my affections are given elsewhere. That would not be fair to either... any of us. It might be a different matter were my affections not already engaged." Even then, he would not have agreed before meeting Lady Elizabeth.

"Hmm. That does rather put a different complexion on things."

"My brother doesn't know that I wish to marry someone else, but he attempted to force my hand anyway." Jack pulled the announcement to the *Gazette* from his pocket and held it out. "I intercepted this before the messenger reached London."

Lord Wellford scowled as he read it. "This would appear to force *my* hand, as well, had I or Elizabeth taken a dislike to you. It was not well done of your brother, to do this before the settlements were signed. Not well done at all, and so I shall tell him when we meet." He handed the paper back. "I take it he only sent the one notice?"

Jack hadn't considered that. Charles would have discovered yesterday that Jack had left Marstone Park—if he suspected what his brother was trying to do, he might well have sent out notices to other papers.

"Ring the bell, Stanlake."

Jack waited until Lord Wellford's secretary had been instructed to contact all the newspaper offices, with instructions to refer any announcements relating to the Wellford family to the marquess before publishing them. Lord Wellford seemed to be in no doubt the various editors would comply.

"Sir, I deeply regret any hurt or distress caused to your daughter. I beg you to believe that my decision is no reflection on her, or you."

"How could it be, Captain, when you had not met either of us? If your brother has spread word of this else-where, to my daughter's detriment, he will come to regret it."

Jack let out a silent breath. It seemed the marquess was more angry with Charles than him.

"If you will excuse me, my lord, I have other business I must attend to. Unless you wish me to explain to Lady—"

"No, no. I will explain to Elizabeth myself. Thank you for your honesty, at least, my boy."

Jack bowed and left, thankful to have got off so lightly. Far from gaining beneficial connections, Charles had started his reign as earl by making a powerful enemy.

Jack pondered his next move as he crossed the square.

Although he had extricated himself from his arranged marriage—unless Charles had managed to get a notice published elsewhere—he was still in no position to ask for Clara's hand. He had no occupation, and no income—Charles would not continue to pay his allowance after learning that his plans had been thwarted. Not only could he not support a wife, but in his current circumstances he could not support himself, either.

A meeting with Clara could only be to explain, and say farewell. Before doing that, he should see if Charles would concede on anything, slim though the chance was.

He would ride back to Marstone Park before calling on Clara. In all honour, Charles should pass on the money from selling his commission—although it appeared honour was in short supply when it came to his brother.

CHAPTER 12

The carriage stopped at the entrance to the narrow cobbled alley of Paternoster Row. It was only a week since Clara had been here in search of reading material, but this time her uncle was with her.

"Look for a sign with a ship," Uncle George said as they alighted. "That's the place we want."

Clara hadn't taken much notice of the signs hanging above the different booksellers' premises on her previous visit, her interest caught by the books displayed in their windows. This time she found it difficult to take an interest in anything.

They had seen Jack in the theatre two nights ago. On the assumption that if he had time to attend the theatre, he would have time to call on her, she had waited indoors all day yesterday. He had not called. Only a great deal of encouragement from Uncle George had persuaded her to accompany him this morning. He was right, she admitted to herself. Spending the day on tenterhooks waiting for the knocker to sound wasn't doing her any good. She wanted to believe Jack had a good reason for staying away, but that became more and more difficult as time passed. For now, she should try to concentrate on Papa's book.

The sign with a ship in full sail was half-way along the street. Uncle George pushed the door open and ushered her in. "We have an appointment with Mr Longman," he said, as a clerk hurried over. "George Morton, and Miss Harper."

The clerk bowed. "Mr Longman is expecting you. Please step this way, sir, miss."

Mr Longman rose as they entered his office, bowed to Clara, and shook Uncle George's hand. "Welcome, sir. I received your letter describing Colonel Harper's work. It could be a useful addition to our list." He indicated a pair of chairs in front of this desk and they sat.

"This is a fair copy." Uncle George placed the parcel of manuscript on the desk before him. "Courtesy of my niece." He inclined his head towards Clara.

"Thank you." Mr Longman unwrapped the package and scanned the first few pages, then returned to the front sheet. "*Edited* by C. Harper?"

Clara didn't care for the surprise in his voice, but she'd promised to let Uncle George do the talking. He was Papa's official representative.

"My niece improved the work greatly," Uncle George said. "My brother-in-law favours long, complex sentences, and has a tendency to repetition. You may also have the unedited manuscript, if you wish, to assess Miss Harper's modifications."

"I beg your pardon, Miss Harper." Mr Longman had a pleasant smile, now with only the faintest hint of condescension. "I will take your word for it, Mr Morton. Now, you understand that the terms I am about to discuss depend on my acceptance of the work, which I will review later. Nothing is contracted until we have a signed document before us."

"As I would expect from a sensible businessman," Uncle George said, and the two men discussed terms and payments while Clara listened.

"That all went very well," her uncle said, when they were out on the street again. "What would you like to do next? Saint Paul's is just down there, should you wish to see it." He pointed to an alley where the dome of the cathedral loomed in the gap between the buildings. "I could return you to Cavendish Square, or you may accompany me to Wapping. I have business at one of my warehouses."

Clara hesitated. They had already been away from home for a couple of hours. If Jack came and she was not—

"If Captain Stanlake should call while you are out and does not return, you are well rid of him," Uncle George said.

He was right; she must hope her feelings would fade, and one way to do that was to turn her mind to other matters. "The warehouse, if you please."

Uncle George nodded, and handed her into the carriage. She hadn't been this far east in London before, and looked out of the carriage windows with interest as they drove along Cheapside, then past the sinister hulk of the tower of London.

"What do you make of young Nolan?" her uncle asked. "He seems friendly, although why he should be so keen on your, and Kitty's, company when he is already betrothed, I do not know."

"He would like a business connection." Clara related what Mr Nolan had said on the *Pegasus*.

"I suspected something of the sort." He glanced at Clara. "Do not think I am offended, my dear. A man has to make connections somehow, and his betrothed seems a pleasant girl. Kitty has taken to her, and it is good that she has friends of her own age."

"Kitty seems to like Miss Templeman's brother, too."

"Should I investigate his background? It would be best to nip a liking in the bud if Templeman is not suitable husband material."

"I'm not sure Kitty has got that far yet in her affections." Unlike her own feelings about Jack. It was more than ten days since she had seen him—surely she should be missing him less by now?

"I will enquire anyway—it may be relevant if I do business with Nolan. Ah, here we are."

The warehouse was not beside the river, but close enough for the smell of salt and mud to be noticeable. Dozens of masts were visible in the gaps between buildings, and she wished she knew where they had all come from, and where they would be sailing to when they had unloaded their cargoes.

Uncle George told his coachman to return for them in an hour, and then led Clara inside. Instantly, her nostrils were assaulted with more pleasant scents of tea and spices. She looked around, but all she saw were piles of boxes and crates, and shelves full of packages in wood and canvas wrappings, with only the enticing smells to show that this place held anything exotic.

"You may listen to my business, although I warn you it will be nothing but discussion of manifests and shipping dates. Or I will send someone to show you around the warehouse." Her uncle must have seen Clara's doubt in her face, as he laughed. "Do not judge by what you see here—there is a showroom, and you may find some of the packages more interesting than they appear."

Uncle George was correct, naturally, and Clara spent a happy hour with her mind on bolts of embroidered silk, fine muslins, dimities, and calicos hand painted or printed in elaborate patterns. There were shelves with blocks of ebony and sandalwood, ready to be made into marquetry or fine furniture, jars of camphor oil and spices—samples that could be touched and smelled. She only thought of Jack five or six times in the hour.

The day after he'd seen Wellford, Jack rode into Marstone Park via the tradesman's gate. A hired horse on a long rein trotted behind Atlas, ready for his departure later. He'd stopped in Hertford for the night, wanting to be well rested before confronting his brother.

The rough track approached the back of the buildings —out of sight of the main parts of the house, which suited Jack perfectly. There were things he wanted to do before encountering Charles. He dismounted in the stable yard, giving Atlas a final pat on the neck as Gibbs hurried towards him.

"Take him for you, sir?"

Jack handed him the reins, and Gibbs led Atlas into a stall. He wasn't gone long.

"His lordship hasn't found out you took Atlas," the stable master said when he reappeared. "Or if he has, he hasn't said anything about it. I wanted him safely back in his stall as soon as possible."

"Good." Charles was going to be furious enough with him—Jack didn't want his brother taking out his temper on the perfectly innocent staff. He indicated the hired horse. "Take care of this fellow, will you? I'm not sure how long I'll be here."

He took the servants' stairs up to his room. Packing the clothing he'd brought back from the Colonies didn't take long, and there was still space in the trunk. He regarded the closet containing clothes he had left behind when he joined the army—most were well out of fashion, but he selected several suits that didn't seem too dated, and folded them into the trunk, then filled the remaining space with shirts, stockings, and neckcloths. Everything smelled strongly of lavender, but the sachets did seem to have kept the moths away, and the aroma would soon wear off. He would send for the rest of his things later, but if Charles' revenge descended to petty levels, he would have something spare with him.

He rang for a footman to take the trunk down to the stables with an instruction to have it sent to the posting inn in Hertford. Then he considered what to do next. Best to say his goodbyes now, in case Charles was incensed enough to have him escorted from the Park. It was still late morning, and the boys would be in the schoolroom.

A Latin lesson was in progress, and he leaned against the door frame while Will finished reciting the declensions of domus. Quite ironic, Jack thought, given that he was likely to be arguing with Charles shortly about who was master.

"I'd like a few minutes with the boys," Jack said, when Will had finished. The tutor bowed and left the room.

"Is something wrong, Uncle Jack?" Will asked.

"I came to say goodbye. I have to go to London."

Will frowned. "You've just been away. Do you really have to go again?"

"It cannot be helped, I'm afraid. And I may be away for a long time, possibly for years." Whether he rejoined the army or had to find some other occupation, he doubted he'd be welcome here for some time. "Think of me when you play in your new fort."

Alfred's lip stuck out. "I won't have much time to play. Now I'm Lord Wingrave, Papa says I need to spend more time learning about family duty. I will be head of the family one day."

"Of course you will, my lord." Jack made a deep bow. Will smirked, but Alfred didn't appear to notice the irony of his gesture.

"Will you write to us, Uncle Jack?" Will asked.

"If I can. Be good, the pair of you."

He descended to the first floor, but hesitated on the landing. Charles would be downstairs in his study, Sarah most likely in her parlour on this floor, as the wind was too cold for her to be sitting in her orchard pavilion. But Charles had warned him to stay away from her. Although he'd been lucky to have avoided notice so far, the chances were high that someone would see him entering or leaving her parlour, and word would get to his brother. He didn't mind incurring Charles' wrath, but his brother would likely take some of his temper out on Sarah.

No—Sarah would understand why he hadn't spoken to her.

When Jack entered the study, Charles was at his desk dictating letters. He gave a triumphant smirk when he saw Jack, and dismissed his secretary.

"Well, Jack, you crept into the Park quietly! Is all settled?"

It seemed Charles hadn't questioned the groom about delivering the notice to the *Gazette*.

"It is, yes." Jack threw the betrothal announcement on the desk. "Wellford was not pleased to find you'd sent this before Lady Elizabeth had a chance to meet me, or to find you'd lied to him."

That wiped the smirk off Charles' face. "Lied?"

"You told him I'd agreed to the match. I told him I had not."

"You told him…? You… you refused the match?"

"I did, and Wellford accepted my reason for doing so." He was not going to explain that—he could imagine the sneer if Charles found out he'd fallen in love with a woman connected to trade. He glanced at the letters book the secretary had left behind. "I do hope you have not informed anyone else of the proposed marriage. Wellford would be seriously displeased, and I suspect you would not wish to upset him further."

"It was Father's wish that—"

"It was his wish that I marry and be happy—as you well know. Your wife and sons may have to do your bidding, but I do not."

"What will you do, then?" Charles' scowl had smoothed.

"Rejoin my regiment, of course." Or some other regiment; it didn't matter which one.

Now Charles was smiling. "But, my dear brother, you have resigned your commission."

"No, you sold my commission, without my knowledge or consent. But I can buy another, and you owe me the money you got for it." He put his hands on the desk and leaned towards his brother, keeping a tight grip on his temper. Charles hurriedly pushed his chair backwards, as if he thought Jack was going to hit him. "Oh, don't worry, dear brother, I shall not soil my hands with you. But if the money is not in my bank account within two days, I'll spread the story of your fraud far and wide." Charles would have to send a messenger with a draft on his own bank, but it could be managed in the time.

Charles' mouth dropped open. "You would not! That would sully your name as well as mine."

Jack's eyes narrowed at his brother's look of horror. Clearly he wanted the appearance of being an honourable man, even if he did not act as one. "I am merely Captain Stanlake of His Majesty's army, Charles. I do not flaunt my connection to the earldom, and my military record speaks for itself. Whereas you have made false claims to both a powerful marquess and someone influential at Horse Guards. Not paying me will add financial fraud to that list—not the act of a gentleman."

Jack kept his eyes on his brother until Charles nodded, his lips compressed.

"Good, we understand each other. In addition, your actions will significantly affect the time I have to spend in England before I can find a regiment to join—and without any pay. You will also advance me a sum to cover my living costs for that period."

"But you're already getting hundreds of—"

"I will need that money to purchase a new commission," Jack interrupted. "If I have to use it for living expenses, I won't be able to afford a commission, in which case I have nothing to lose by spreading word of your perfidy." He wouldn't do so, for that might eventually harm Alfred and Will, but Charles' resigned expression showed he thought it was possible.

"Oh, very well. But do not show your face here again."

"Two hundred should cover it."

"Two—?" Charles' scowl deepened.

"Family honour, Charlie," Jack said softly. "In my bank, within two days." Then he turned and walked out.

CHAPTER 13

*J*ack presented himself in Cavendish Square the following morning, the skies and drizzle as grey as his mood. After riding the hired hack into Hertford, he'd taken the stage to London and found a cheap room for the night. He had to eke out his meagre reserves of money until Charles' draft arrived at the bank. If Charles sent it at all.

So here he was, scrubbed and in his least unfashionable suit, about to explain why he hadn't called, and then to say goodbye to the woman he loved and would marry if he could. The easiest course would be to avoid her altogether, so he did not have to remind himself of what he would be losing. But he'd said he would call, and he must. The compulsion to see her one last time was inescapable, no matter the cost.

Perhaps he was imagining his feelings, a logical part of his mind said, but he didn't think so.

The butler showed him into a parlour, saying that he

thought the ladies were out but that Mr Morton would see him.

It was for the best, he told himself. Morton was a perceptive man and probably guessed something of how he felt. He would explain his situation and take his leave.

He turned as the door opened—it wasn't Morton, but Clara. He took a step towards her, wanting to take her in his arms, but her expression, as well as his own situation, stopped him. He thought he'd seen a quick smile, but that had now gone and she didn't appear to be as happy to see him as he was to see her. That was probably just as well, for her sake.

"Captain, what brings you here now?" She remained in the doorway.

"I... That is, did your trunk arrive safely?" He didn't care about the trunk, but the words of apology he'd rehearsed depended on her being pleased to see him.

"It did, thank you." She smiled, but it was a stiff, formal thing. "I was sorry to hear about your father. Uncle George saw the notice in the *Gazette*."

"He had a good life," Jack said. "It's never easy, when someone dies."

"I suppose you were kept busy in Hertfordshire?"

"I was, in somewhat unexpected ways. I know... I think you saw me in the theatre. I wanted to call then... I wanted to very much, but there were reasons I could not do so until now. Please, will you let me explain?" He almost held his breath while she considered her answer— it would make no practical difference to their future, but he didn't want to part with her thinking ill of him.

. . .

Clara felt the lump of unhappiness inside her begin to dissipate. Something was wrong beyond the loss of his father.

"I am pleased you have come, Jack. I missed our conversations. But what is amiss? What has happened?" She crossed the room to stand before him.

"Clara, I…" He took a deep breath and started again. "My circumstances have changed. I had hoped to ask you to come with me—to ask if you would think about living as a soldier's wife. I know your father is permanently based in Albany, but you must have some idea what life would be like following a regiment. I would often be absent, even if we were both on the same side of the Atlantic."

Clara's breath caught at the beginning of his speech. He did want her as she wanted him! But then she recognised the true meaning of his words—he wasn't asking her to marry him, but wishing he were in a position to do so.

He reached out a hand, as if to touch her face, but then dropped it and moved away. "I shouldn't have spoken. I have even less now than I had before—my brother sold my commission without my knowledge or permission. And he hasn't said so, but he is certain to stop my allowance. Army pay… well, it's barely sufficient for normal expenses, let alone for a wife and family."

The brother he mentioned would be the new Earl of Marstone—a man with rank and power.

"At present, I'm no longer in the army, so with no pay and no allowance either."

Clara listened in growing dismay and then relief as he described the events of the last few days. Financial problems could be addressed, but an unwanted betrothal—there would have been no going back from that if the Marquess of Wellford had not been so understanding.

"Can you not buy another commission?"

"I have an appointment next week at Horse Guards with someone who should be able to deal with it, but..." He shrugged. "My brother can be vindictive."

"If he sold your commission once without your permission, he might do so again, or even prevent you purchasing another now."

"Those were my thoughts, yes." He rubbed his forehead. "I have no other skills, and I am too old to start thinking of taking up the law, or going into the church."

"I cannot imagine you preaching from a pulpit." She should have held her tongue—it sounded as if she were making light of his predicament. But his expression brightened, and he almost laughed.

"It's clear I'm not suited to that, is it not? But what else?"

He had gone from amusement back to dejection—with good reason—but she did not think giving up so easily was part of his character. And this would be her future, too, now.

"Jack, when battle plans go amiss, what do you do? Surrender?"

"No." He stood up straighter. "Revise the plan, or retreat and regroup so another attack can be made. But if this were a battle, Charles has more troops. If I cannot rejoin the British Army, I suppose there are others who require a soldier's skills."

He sounded as if he were talking to himself, but it gave Clara an idea. She recalled one of the first conversations she'd had with him. "When outnumbered in a strange country, take advice from your native allies."

He frowned. "Native…? I'm not in a strange country."

"You are in the realm of the influence bestowed by wealth and rank, and possibly of legal battles. Those things are strange to you, are they not?"

He began to look interested. "The legal battles, certainly."

"They are not strange to Uncle George—they are a large part of his business. If he cannot assist you, I'm sure he knows other people who can. Would you share your story with him?"

"If you think he can help, yes. But Clara…" His words tailed off, and he suddenly looked uncertain. "What I said before. Would you… I mean, do you… can you return my regard?"

"Yes." The word came out without thought, and she took a step towards him.

Jack stepped away, and put his hands behind his back. "I should not… I mean, not until—"

"Stop talking, Jack." Daringly, she put out a finger and held it across his lips. "You… We… are not going to let your brother spoil our lives, are we? So although we do not yet know how to resolve the situation, we *do* know that we will. Do we not?"

His smile held tenderness… and something else. That expression she'd seen in the storm. She felt suddenly breathless.

"We will resolve it somehow." One hand came up to cup her face and he bent his head until his mouth met hers. It was a strange feeling at first, lovely, but nothing to the warmth that spread through her when her lips parted and the kiss deepened. The hard pressure of his chest against hers, and his hands on her back and in her hair, felt... exciting. Something with the promise of much more.

Jack reluctantly pulled himself away at the sound of a throat being cleared. Loudly. And he felt himself blushing like a schoolboy at the sight of George Morton's raised brows.

"I do hope the two of you have some happy news for me," he said, in a voice that almost sounded stern, but not quite.

"Happy intentions, sir, rather than news. The matter is not straightforward."

"I sense a tale to be told," Morton said. "Best come into the library. Anne and Kitty are likely to return at any moment, and I would rather discuss the matter without their raptures."

Raptures? But Morton had left the room already, Clara behind him, so Jack had to follow.

"A plain tale, if you please," Morton said, when the three of them were seated.

Jack told his story, twice. The second time, at Morton's insistence, he gave all the details of his father's wishes, and the parts of the will pertaining to himself. Morton nodded at intervals.

"Tell me, Captain, would you be offering for Clara if your father were still alive?"

Would he? The question was no longer relevant, but he had been thinking of doing so even before his father died.

"Yes. Why should the two of us be made unhappy to satisfy my father's sense of what is due to the family?" He glanced at Clara, who was looking at her hands folded in her lap. "And now Father has gone, family duty no longer applies. My brother's actions have negated any obligation I might have felt to conform to his wishes."

"And you, Clara. Does the fact that you are likely to be estranged from your husband's family matter?"

Clara shook her head. "You know that a title, or titled relatives, were Mama's ambition, Uncle. Never mine."

"There remains the matter of making a living, sir," Jack said. "As Clara pointed out, my brother could still adversely affect my army career."

"If you were in the King's army, yes."

The prospect of selling his services to some other country did not sit well with him—but what other army was there? Then his eye was caught by the tiger rug.

The East India Company had an army—serving there would still be serving his country, in a way.

"Would someone like my brother have influence in the East India Company's army?"

Morton smiled. "He may or may not, but *I* have a great deal of influence there. I understand they are expanding the army, and a man with your experience would be welcome. You might be able to join as a major, or even higher. Should I make enquiries on your behalf?"

"I…" He was about to accept, but asking Clara to share a life in India with him was very different from returning to the Colonies. Hot and disease-ridden, from what he had heard.

"I would love to see India," she said, as if she had read his mind.

"That is not your only option, Stanlake," Morton said. "You are a landowner, don't forget."

"Charles will not release those estates."

"He will if the law requires it."

"That might take years, and money I do not have," Jack objected.

"Years, yes. But if you had an agent in England, with a power of attorney to deal with the matter on your behalf —what then?"

Could it be as easy as that?

"I would be willing to act in that capacity, if you wish," Morton went on. "I will check the exact terms of the will at Doctor's Commons, but if it is as you say, then I am prepared to take the risk of losing. Call it a joint venture, if you will." He stood. "I will leave the two of you to discuss your options."

Clara felt as dazed as Jack looked. "It seems that Uncle George *can* help."

He didn't appear so sure. "How much do you know about India?"

"Not a great deal. Not yet, at least. But I would love to find out." She thought he would tell her it wasn't a suitable place for women, so his next words surprised her.

"We may get there and you—or I, I suppose—find we do not like it after all. Or you may become ill."

She went to stand beside him and put a hand on his arm. "Jack?"

He took her hands. "India looks impressive, doesn't it, in the illustrations you see in books—palatial buildings, exotic clothing... But they don't show the heat and the flies, the diseases, hostile natives. I don't want to risk your health—"

"There were hostile natives aplenty in the Colonies, and disease is everywhere. Besides, what of yourself? I will have to worry about you dying in battle in addition to all those other dangers. It is a foolish thing, falling in love with a soldier, but it is too late for me to think of that now."

His fingers tightened on hers. "You do love me, then?"

How could a man like him appear so uncertain? "Of course I do; did I not say so?" She moved a step closer. "Jack, if India does not agree with us, we will decide together what to do. And whatever we do, your brother will not bother us any longer."

"I will have won in more ways than escaping his influence," he said, with a wry smile. "Not only will he have no power over me, but your uncle will wrest my estates from his grasp."

"And you are marrying against his wishes," she added.

"Your wishes are the important ones here, and mine." And to her great delight, he proceeded to demonstrate again how their wishes for each other would be satisfied.

EPILOGUE

Calcutta, India, three years later

Clara stoppered her bottle of ink and left the pages to dry thoroughly, weighted down against the gentle wafting of the ceiling fan. That was her letter to Uncle George ready to be sent on the next merchantman, together with a parcel of fabric samples and carved trinkets. She would enclose Jack's letter to Will with it— Uncle George had worked out a way to get an occasional missive to the lad without the earl finding out. Jack would have liked to write to Alfred as well, but couldn't be sure that he wouldn't tell his father.

She smoothed the fine muslin of her gown—scandalously thin if she were to wear it in public, especially without stays and stockings. But this was her private room, and only her ayah would see her like this. And Jack, of course.

Kitty—now Mrs Templeman—had written that the fabric was proving popular for married ladies, and Clara had laughed at the turn of phrase. She saw the way Jack's eyes lit up when she wore it in the bedchamber, and wondered if Kitty had seen the same expression on her husband's face. Kitty's last letter had carried the news that her husband had at last bought a house in the countryside. Now she could get on with making a rose garden and putting down roots, just in time for the birth of her first child. That missive had been dated four months ago, so Clara was probably already an aunt.

Uncle George's letter had said only that importing the fabric had been very profitable, and would she please concentrate on finding more suppliers of new goods. She was planning a trip with Jack to Dacca when he had some leave—it would be lovely to spend time together, and would also allow her to investigate the production there of muslins, dimities, and calicos. Dacca was reputed to be where the best examples of such fabrics were to be obtained. She would visit the bazaar there, too, in the hope of discovering another craftsman like the one who had carved the ivory elephant on her desk. He now worked with jewels and other rich materials beyond his wildest dreams, and had an increasing number of employees—and Uncle George had an exclusive supplier of ornamental brooches, snuff boxes, and paperweights that were making a tidy profit. Business was so much more interesting than growing roses!

Jack was due back in an hour, so it was time she dressed for the governor's party. She was moving in higher circles than she'd anticipated. On reaching India, Jack hadn't spent long with his initial regiment. He'd shown an aptitude for dealing with native officials and rulers, and had quickly been seconded to the governor's office here in Calcutta. That change had given her the chance to develop her business interests, so both of them were happy at the way things had turned out. She wouldn't be surprised if Jack eventually rose to a high position within the governance of the East India Company.

On her way to her bedchamber Clara looked into the little room they used as a nursery. George was asleep beneath the mosquito netting, one thumb stuck firmly in his mouth. The nursemaid sitting in the corner with some mending bobbed her head—all was well—and Clara crept out quietly. Their son had exceedingly powerful lungs, and she had no desire for him to demonstrate the fact now.

Her ayah was finishing her hair when Jack came into the room. The ayah placed the last pins, then left them.

"You look lovely, as always." Jack stood behind her, his hand playing with one of the ringlets draped over her shoulder.

She slapped his hand away with a laugh and turned to face him. "Don't make Kala have to do my hair again. You're earlier than I expected."

"I am. We have enough time to go via the river, if you are ready? It will be cooler."

"That would be lovely." Cooler, and also more peaceful than travelling the crowded streets in a carriage.

Jack eyed the muslin gown lying across the bed. "You can put that on again when we get home," he said, lifting a fold of the filmy fabric, with a look in his eyes that made her shiver with anticipation.

"I'm sure that can be arranged." Although it was what came after wearing the gown that they were both antic-ipating.

THE

CUSTOMS AND HABITS

OF THE

WOMEN OF INDIA

with particular notes on the ftyles
of clothing and cofmetics

by C. STANLAKE

author of
The Cafte Syftem Explained
Life in a Seraglio
Anecdotes of a Year in Madras
and
The Methods of Manufacture of Indian Muflins

LONDON

PRINTED FOR THOS. LONGMAN

PATERNOSTER ROW

1778

Thank you for reading *A Question of Duty*; I hope you enjoyed it. If you can spare a few minutes, I'd be very grateful if you could review this book on Amazon or Goodreads.

A Question of Duty is a prequel novella for the *Marstone Series*.

Seventeen years after the events in this story, the Earl of Marstone's elder son has died, leaving Will as his heir. The earl is determined that his brother Jack will not inherit the title under any circumstances.

Sauce for the Gander (Book 1 in the *Marstone Series*) is the story of what happens when he attempts to ensure this.

Read on to find out more about the *Marstone Series*.

My website has more details about this series and my other stories.

www.jaynedavisromance.co.uk

If you want news of special offers or new releases, join my mailing list via the contact page on my website. I won't bombard you with emails, I promise! Alternatively, follow me on Facebook - links are on my website.

THE MARSTONE SERIES

A duelling viscount, a courageous poor relation and an overbearing lord—just a few of the characters you will meet in The Marstone Series. From windswept Devonshire, to Georgian London and revolutionary France, true love is always on the horizon and shady dealings often afoot.

The series is named after Will, who eventually becomes the 9th Earl of Marstone. He appears in all the stories, although often in a minor role.

Each book can be read as a standalone story, but readers of the series will enjoy meeting characters from previous books.

They are all available on Kindle (including Kindle Unlimited) and in paperback. The four full-length novels are also available as an ebook box set.

A duel. An ultimatum. An arranged marriage.

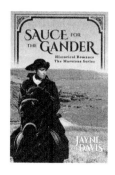

England, 1777

Will, Viscount Wingrave, whiles away his time gambling and bedding married women, thwarted in his wish to serve his country by his controlling father. News that his errant son has fought a duel with a jealous husband is the last straw for the Earl of Marstone. He decrees that Will must marry. The earl's eye lights upon Connie Charters, daughter of a poor but socially ambitious father.

Connie wants a husband who will love and respect her, not a womaniser and a gambler. When her conniving father forces the match, she has no choice but to agree.

Will and Connie meet for the first time at the altar. As they settle into their new home on the wild coast of Devonshire, the young couple find they have more in common than they thought. But there are dangerous secrets that threaten both them and the nation.

Can Will and Connie overcome the dark forces that conspire against them and find happiness together?

ABOUT THE AUTHOR

I wanted to be a writer when I was in my teens, hooked on Jane Austen and Georgette Heyer (and lots of other authors). Real life intervened, and I had several careers, including as a non-fiction author under another name. That wasn't *quite* the writing career I had in mind!

Now I am lucky enough to be able to spend most of my time writing, when I'm not out walking, cycling, or enjoying my garden.

Printed in Great Britain
by Amazon